❧ Ida B ❧

Ida B

... and Her Plans to Maximize Fun,
Avoid Disaster, and
(Possibly) Save the World

Katherine Hannigan

A Greenwillow Book
■ HarperTrophy®
An Imprint of HarperCollinsPublishers

Library of Congress Cataloging-in-Publication Data
Hannigan, Katherine.
Ida B . . . and her plans to maximize fun, avoid disaster, and (possibly)
save the world / by Katherine Hannigan.
 p. cm.
"Greenwillow Books."
Summary: Fourth-grader Ida B spends happy hours being home-
schooled and playing in her family's apple orchard, until circumstances
force her parents to sell part of the orchard and send her to public
school.
ISBN-13: 978-0-06-073024-6 (trade bdg.) ISBN-10: 0-06-073024-2
(trade bdg.)
ISBN-13: 978-0-06-073025-3 (lib. bdg.) ISBN-10: 0-06-073025-0
(lib. bdg.)
ISBN-13: 978-0-06-073026-0 (pbk.) ISBN-10: 0-06-073026-9 (pbk.)
[1. Family life—Wisconsin—Fiction. 2. Schools—Fiction.
3. Nature—Fiction. 4. Sick—Fiction. 5. Cancer—Fiction.
6. Orchards—Fiction. 7. Wisconsin—Fiction.] I. Title.
PZ7.H19816Id 2004 [Fic]—dc22 2003035625

The text of this book is set in 13-point Perpetua.
Typography by Paul Zakris

First Harper Trophy edition, 2007

For the hills and the trees, the wind,
the rivers, and the stars.
And for Victor.
Always—K.H.

Chapter 1

"Ida B," Mama said to me on one of those days that start right and just keep heading toward perfect until you go to sleep, "when you're done with the dishes, you can go play. Daddy and I are going to be working till dinner."

"Yes, ma'am," I said back, but I said it like this, "Yes, MAY-uhm!" because I couldn't wait to get on with my business. I could already hear the brook calling to me through the back door screen. "C'mon out and play, Ida B. Hurry up, hurry up, hurry up." I had three places I wanted to visit, six things I wanted to make, and two conversations I hoped to have before dinnertime.

Mama was washing, Daddy was drying, and I was putting away the dishes from lunch. And I knew that the moment I set the last pan in its place, I was free. But the way those two were chatting and laughing and acting like we had till next week to finish up, I could see it was going to be a while.

My insides started itching and my feet started hopping, one then the other, because they were ten minutes past being ready to go. So I decided to speed things up a bit.

Daddy'd hand me a dish, I'd sprint to the cupboard and put it away, race back again, and put my hand out for the next one, with my right foot tap, tap, tapping the seconds that were ticking by.

"Hold your horses, Ida B," Daddy told me. "There's plenty of time to do whatever you're planning." And he passed me a plate, slow and easy.

Well, that stopped me in my tracks. Because what Daddy said might have seemed all right to him, but it was sitting about two miles beyond wrong with me. I wasn't going to be able to put away another tiny teaspoon till I set things straight.

"Daddy," I said, and I waited till he was looking at me before I went on.

"Yes, Ida B," he answered, turning toward me.

And staring right into his eyeballs I told him, "There is never enough time for fun."

Daddy's eyes opened wide, and for a half second I wondered if I was in for something close to trouble. But then the two ends of his mouth turned up, just a little.

"Ida B," he told the ceiling while he shook his head.

"Hmmmmm," Mama said, like a smile would sound if it could.

And as soon as Daddy handed me the big frying pan, I set it in the drawer next to the oven, and I was on my way.

"Come on, Rufus," I called to Daddy's old floppy-eared dog, who was napping under the table. "You can come, too, so you'll have some company."

Now, a school of goldfish could go swimming in the pool of drool that dog makes while he's sleeping. But as soon as he heard his name and saw me heading for outside he jumped up, cleaned up the extra slobber around his mouth, and in two and one-half seconds' time, he was waiting for me at the back door.

❦ Chapter 2 ❦

On my way out of the house, I grabbed a pencil and enough paper to make four good drawings and one mistake. And in my right pants pocket, I stuffed some string to tie the sticks together for the rafts I build and send down the brook with notes attached to them saying things like:

> What is life like in Canada?
> Please respond.

Ida B. Applewood
P.O. Box 42
Lawson's Grove, Wisconsin 55500

or

If this raft reaches the ocean,
will you please let us know?
Thank you very much.

Applewood Raft
Construction Company
P.O. Box 42
Lawson's Grove, Wisconsin 55500

It is my belief that the brook ends up at one of those two places, but I haven't heard anything back yet to prove that. The best I've gotten so far is some old man from way up in Roaring Forks called up Mama and Daddy and told them I was sending out notes with my name and address on them and they might want to discourage that.

And a teacher from Myers Falls, which is the next town over, got ahold of one of my notes and made her whole class find out things about Canada. Boring things like, "There are thirty-two million people," and "Some of Canada's main exports are timber and aluminum," and they sent all those facts and figures to me in an envelope.

Mama made me write a thank-you note back, so I drew a picture of a Canadian Mountie holding the Queen of England in his arms and they're going over Niagara Falls in a wooden barrel, waving aluminum maple leaves, just screaming with glee. "Thank you very much for the information," I wrote. "Let's all hope they're having some fun over in Canada, too. Yours truly, Ida B. Applewood."

So I had my string, my paper, Daddy's dog, and three pieces of bubble gum so I could blow a bubble as big as my face while being careful to keep it away from Rufus, because the last time he got near one of those, we were cutting pink gum out of his fur for about a month after. And I headed out to the apple orchard.

"Hello, Beulah. Hello, Charlie. Hello, Pastel," I said, which are some of the names I've given those trees. All of the apple trees were full of blossoms, and when you stood right in the middle of them you could smell their prettiness, but not so much it'd bother you.

I was already sitting down under Henry VIII, getting to work on a drawing I'd started the day before. It was the orchard after the harvest, with bushels of apples under all of the trees. There were Mama and Daddy, me, Lulu the cat, and Rufus, each sitting in our own tree, eating slices of apple pie. I was working on Rufus, who had a mix of slobber and crumbs all over him, and Lulu was giving him a look of the utmost revulsion, when I realized that not one of those trees had said anything back to me.

Now, some people might stop me right there and say, "Ida B, you could wait for eternity and a day and you're not going to hear one of those trees talking to you, let alone a brook. Trees don't have mouths, and they don't speak, and you might want to take yourself to the doctor's and get a very thorough check-up real soon."

And after I took a minute to give my patience and forbearance a chance to recover my mouth from the rudeness that was itching to jump out of it, I would just say this: "There's more than one way to tell each other things, and there's more than one way to listen, too. And if you've never heard a tree telling you something, then I'd say you don't really know how to listen just yet. But I'd be happy to give you a few pointers sometime."

So I gave those trees another chance to reply and hollered, "I said, 'Hello,' everybody. Didn't you hear me?"

But instead of the usual chorus of "Hi"s and "Hey there"s, only Viola said, "How are you doing today, Ida B?"

"I'm just fine on such a getting-to-perfect

day," I said. "What's the matter with everybody? Why are you all so quiet?"

But they stayed silent. Even the loud ones. Especially the rude ones.

"Hey, what's going on?" I yelled.

Finally I heard Gertrude whisper, "You tell her, Viola."

"All right," Viola whispered back, very discreetly.

Viola hemmed and hawed for a bit, though. "Well . . . " she started, and "Hmmm . . . ahhh . . . ummm . . . " she tried again until she finally got something out. "Ida B, how's everything going at home? How's your fam—"

But before she could finish, that punk Paulie T. was interrupting. "We heard a rumor that something bad's headed your way, Ida B." And if trees could grin like jack-o'-lanterns with bad intentions, that's what Paulie T. would have been doing right then.

"And who told you that, Paulie T.?" I asked,

because I didn't trust him with a thimbleful of water, let alone the truth.

"I'm not revealing my sources," he said.

"Did you hear something, Viola? How about you, Beatrice? Or is Paulie T. just talking out of his branches?"

"Ida B, don't pay him any mind," Viola told me. "We heard something on the wind about a storm headed your way, and we were all settling in and hoping you were okay, too. That's all."

"There's no storm coming today," I said. "Can't you feel how beautiful it is?"

"You take care of yourself now, Ida B," said Viola. And then they all just stood there, like they were sleeping standing up.

Well, I got tired of feeling like I was alone in that particular crowd, and I was peeved about Paulie T.'s pleasure at my expense. "All right then, I'm headed off to have some fun somewhere else," I said.

And none of them said a word back.

Once Rufus and I got to the brook, I asked right off, "Did you hear something about me and some trouble?"

"Did you bring the rafts? Are you ready to play? Get 'em ready and get 'em in so we can play, Ida B," said the brook, ignoring my question.

"In a minute. First I want to know if you heard something about trouble heading my way."

"My-oh-my, and will you look at that," the brook replied. "I'm late for an appointment, Ida B. Gotta go, gotta go.

"Better talk to the old tree," the brook went on as it rolled away. "Yep, yep, that's a good idea," it called as it tumbled over the rocks and around the mountain and was gone.

Now, by that time I'd just about lost my patience with the bunch of them. But talking to the old tree was a good piece of advice, so I didn't mind the brook's rudeness too much.

Rufus and I hiked up the mountain—which isn't really a mountain, but "hill" is just too tiny a word for it—till we got to the old tree that has no leaves and hardly any bark. That tree's bare and white, and people think it's dead but it's not; it's just older than old. It hardly ever speaks, and even if it does you often have to wait awhile. But when it does you want to listen, because it's also wiser than wise. And it always tells the truth, unlike some of the young trees that tell you what they think you want to hear or are just too, too clever.

When we got in front of the old tree I said, "There's a rumor around that I'm in for some trouble. Now that's from Paulie T., and you and I both know that his word's worth about two fake pennies. But I was wondering if there's something I need to know?"

Then I climbed up into the tree's branches, and Rufus settled in down at the bottom of the trunk. I rested my head on one of the limbs, closed my eyes, and got ready to listen with my insides, because that's what you have to do with that particular tree.

I was sitting there for quite a while, and not minding a bit. The branch against my face was warm and smooth, and it still felt like a nothing-could-go-wrong day. I was ready to believe that Paulie T. had just been working his mischief, when all of a sudden I got a cold feeling inside of me and I saw a dark cloud at the front of my closed eyes.

And I got a message, but not in words. That tree lets you know things, those things go into your heart, then they find their way up to your head, and once they get there they turn into words. At least that's how I think it works. So, if I had to give it words, this is what I'd say the tree was telling me:

"Hard times are coming."

Well, my eyes flipped open so I wouldn't have to look at that darkness anymore. I jumped out of the tree, almost landing on Rufus the Saliva Factory, because I felt like I'd gotten a shock right through me.

"What?" I asked. "What did you tell me?"

But the old tree is slow to speak, and it doesn't repeat itself. It just stood there, like those apple trees had before.

"Are you telling me that Paulie T. is right? Is trouble heading my way?"

But I knew I wouldn't hear anything back. And on a day like that, with the sun shining, four hours till dinner, and seven more items on my List of Fun Stuff to Do, I did the only sensible thing. I decided that the old tree might not be thinking as well as it had a few years ago. Agreeing with Paulie T. was a sure sign that something was wrong. But I wanted to be respectful and not say anything insulting.

"Well, thanks for helping me out," I yelled as I started running—down the hill, over the brook, through the orchard, and all the way home. I finished my drawings in my room, safe and out of the way, just in case a storm did blow through.

Except for a dinner that included lima beans and brussels sprouts, nothing bad happened that night or the next day. We did have a storm, with thunder and lightning, a couple of days later. It was a wild ruckus outside with leaves and branches blowing by and Lulu hiding under the bed trying to pretend she wasn't scared, just curious about those dust balls.

And that, I believed, was what all those trees were talking about. No need, I figured, to bother my head about it again.

⚜ Chapter 3 ⚜

"Eyedabee." This is how Mama and Daddy and anybody who knows me particularly well say my name. My mama's name is Ida, and even though our names are near-to-identical, my daddy says them real different.

Most of the time when Daddy says "Ida B," it's fast and it's smiling and goes up and down real quick, like tapping your feet to some happy music.

But when he says "Ida," that name stretches on and on, with no rough edges or sharp turns. "Eyhhh-dah," he says, and his breath travels around the room, slips across Mama's shoulders, then her waist, and it keeps going out and about so that everybody gets wrapped in its warm softness. You can still hear it in your head after the sound has stopped, and you're smiling just because somebody said the word "Ida," which isn't even the prettiest name in the world.

The only time I'm anything other than "Ida B" at home is if I'm in trouble. If that's the case—and it has occurred on an occasion or two—and my folks are yelling for me, it's "IDA B. APPLE-WOOD." All the words are broken up, like they're getting hammered out: "IDA . . . B . . . APPLEWOOD . . . Where are you? You come on home!"

Then, wherever I am, sitting in the old tree up on the mountain or building a dam in the brook,

I'll say, "Well, that's me. Guess I'll get going."

If I'm in the orchard, the older apple trees will tell me, "You'd better get a move on, Ida B" or "Go on now and see what your daddy wants."

But the brook always whines and wheedles: "Don't go, Ida B, don't go. Nobody's callin' and they can wait, anyway. Stay, Ida B. Stay and play."

I don't get in trouble for too much. Most of the time it's just little things: it was my turn to put the dishes away and I forgot, or I fed the leftover succotash to the poor and starving wild animals in the neighborhood.

Once I made a house for Lulu out of a whole bunch of books and boxes. I started in the middle of the living room with the biggest box for Lulu's Private Quarters. It had a whisk for a TV antenna and a cushion from the sofa for a bed, and I cut out windows with the big, sharp knife. I built a library, a playroom, and a dining room with some of the other boxes. I made apartments under the chairs and tables with sheets and blankets covering them up like tents so all of her friends-that-she-might-have-someday-when-she-improves-her-attitude could come and visit. It got so big it took up almost the whole living room and was spilling into the hallway.

And Lulu was so pleased she almost purred.

But then Lulu got bored and went outside and I went with her, and pretty soon I heard "IDA B. APPLEWOOD!" down by the brook.

So I got on home and put everything away. But it was a sad thing to have to close up the Lulu and Her Someday Friends' Big City High-Rise and Exotic Resort.

Another time I caused a stir and got Mama and Daddy upset but not too mad was when I invented The Soap Mask.

Now, you probably know that for every

world-famous, history-changing invention ever created, first there was a problem that needed to be solved. My problem was this: too much washing up, of my face in particular.

When I got up in the morning, I'd have to wash my face and hands. And before I could eat my supper or go to the store or go visiting, I'd have to wash them again. It seemed like just about every time I'd get excited and want to get on with life I'd have to stop and wash up. And by the time I was done with it, who knows what opportunities had passed me by.

So I was thinking I would save a lot of time and energy if I could figure out a way to keep my face clean, and The Soap Mask is what I came up with. "An impenetrable wall of disinfectant for your face." "A shield that repels germs while it gently cleanses your pores, leaving a spanking-clean exterior." "Eternal, perpetual, ultimate cleanliness." That's what the advertisements would say, I was thinking, when I put it on the market and sold ten million of them.

Bar soap, I knew, would not work for this project. First off, if you wet it and slather it on, it's white and foamy and would just look silly. Plus I didn't think it would be strong enough. I wanted a powerful solution.

Now, here's what's great about dish soap: it spreads around real well but it also sticks in one place; it will dry if it's left out in the air for a while; it is very strong; it is antibacterial. Perfect.

After supper one night I took a bottle of our best dishwashing liquid to the upstairs bathroom, closed the door, and smeared a thin layer of the stuff all over my face. Then I sat in my room and felt the liquid slowly drying, getting tighter and tighter, joining with my skin so that my entire face was being transformed into a grime repellent. And I left that soap on all night, too, so its dirt-and disease-killing properties had time to really settle in.

In the morning my face looked scrubbed, like I'd washed it with steel wool. It was red and shiny and kind of pinched looking. It itched and burned something close to fierce, but I just chalked that up to the The Mask's potent power.

I went to the table for breakfast and smiled real big every time I said, "Please pass the milk" or "Please pass a napkin." And I waited for Mama and Daddy to notice my gleam.

Finally, after I'd asked for the milk twice when I didn't need it, there were Mama and Daddy both staring at me, with their mouths wide open. And I was sure it was because of their awe and amazement at my bright sparkliness.

"Evan, do you see that?" Mama said. "She's turning bright red and then white, red and white, like a neon sign."

"I see it, Ida," Daddy said back.

Then everything happened so fast I didn't have a chance to get a word out. Mama said something about scarlet fever, Daddy said something else about mumps or chicken pox, Mama was calling the doctor, Daddy was wrapping me up in a blanket and putting me in the truck. Next thing, we were all driving into town and they were so quiet and tense it just seemed like it was not a good time to speak, let alone talk about my groundbreaking, earth-shattering invention.

Well, we got in to see the doctor pretty quick. She looked over just about every part of me, and then she asked me, "Ida B, did you do something to your face?" So I told her all about The Soap Mask.

She listened real closely, and then she said, "Ida B, your skin's turning colors and you're feeling like your face is on fire because the dish soap has irritated it. So we're going to rinse it off, I'm going to give you some lotion to soothe your skin, and it should be back to normal in no time."

Then she gave me a big smile and said, "But no more masks of dish soap, all right?"

Now, even though it might not have worked out as well as I'd planned, I believed the doctor was telling me that The Soap Mask, minus the dish soap, was still an excellent idea worth exploring, so I was encouraged. And she was saying that the flashes of flame that kept engulfing my face from the inside out would soon be extinguished with a real simple solution.

"All right," I said, and I smiled and looked at Mama and Daddy.

Up to this point, they were real nervous looking. They were holding hands and staring hard at me, then the doctor.

But while the doctor was talking to me, they were transformed. First, Mama let out a big sigh, and Daddy smiled and shook his head. Then Daddy picked me up and said, "Oh, Ida B," and Mama hugged both of us. We were having a Thank Goodness Ida B's All Right Celebration right then and there, and all that was missing were cake and presents.

After we were done hugging each other, and hugging the doctor, and shaking the receptionist's hand, we got in the truck to go home.

Before Daddy started the engine, though, Mama turned to me and said, real serious, "Ida B, a trip to the doctor is expensive, so you always need to tell us if something's wrong or if it's not, okay?"

I made my brow furrow and my eyes big just like hers so she'd know I was serious, too. "Okay, Mama," I said.

But in my head I was thinking this: that if a child waited to speak until all the grown-ups settled down and gave her some room to say her piece, most important things would never get said.

Chapter 4

On nights when he was done with the day's work, and we were full up from dinner, and Rufus was moping about hoping for some company and travel, and the stars were all out shining and looking like they were so close you could pick them, Daddy might say, "Ida B, let's take Rufus and go look at the world while it's sleeping."

"All right, Daddy," I'd say back. And we'd head

out through the fields and orchard and around the base of the mountain, Rufus running ahead seeing how many things he could stick his nose into in one night without getting stuck back or stung or sprayed.

This was when my daddy would tell me deep and abiding truths. So I'd try to stay as still as someone like me can, and listen.

One night as we were walking along, Daddy took a deep breath, the kind that sounds like you're smelling something when the air's going in and you're sighing when the air's coming out, and it means something important's about to be spoken.

"Ida B," he said, to make sure I was paying attention.

"Yes, Daddy." I let him know that I was.

"I want you to think about something."

"All right."

Daddy stopped walking, and then I stopped

walking. Because sometimes if you're saying something deep and abiding, you want saying it to be the only thing you're doing, and listening to it to be the only thing the other person's doing. We both looked straight ahead at the fields and the mountain and the sky. And then he began.

"Ida B, some day this land is going to be yours."

"Yes, Daddy."

"And the law is going to say that you own this land and you can do pretty much what you want with it."

"Yes, Daddy," I said again, because I knew he wasn't going to go on till I talked, too. Like in church when the minister waits for you to say "Amen" before he gets on with his preaching.

"But I want you to remember this: We don't own the earth. We are the earth's caretakers, Ida B." Here he took another one of those deep breaths. "I'm grateful we have this land and grateful that you'll have it, too. But we don't own it. We take care of it and all of the things on it. And when we're done with it, it should be left better than we found it."

Now, you should know that my daddy is a very intelligent man. Most of the time we don't disagree about much, except things like bedtime and whether children should be forced to eat certain foods. So while I agreed with most of what he said, I was thinking he might want to reconsider one of his ideas. And I was just the person to help him do that.

When Daddy talks like that, though, I don't say anything right away. He looked so serious when he said it, "We are the earth's caretakers, Ida B," staring off into the sky, wiping his brow, and nodding. I knew I needed to wait a bit before I shared Ida B's Golden and Supremely Important Nugget of Wisdom. So we walked for a while.

But when we were headed back toward home and we got to the orchard, I said, "Daddy?"

"Yes, Ida B."

"I do believe there are enough apples growing in that orchard that we could have pie every day of the week, and send a few to the Queen of England, as well."

"Hmmm," Daddy said.

I gave him a few minutes to ponder that thought.

When we were passing by the brook I said, "Daddy?"

"Yes, Ida B."

"Sometimes in the summer I'll get to sweating and stinking so bad that Lulu will hiss at me when I get near her and even Rufus will run away. So I'll come on over here and lie down in the brook with my clothes still on. I'll let its coolness roll over me and I'll feel the stink rolling away, too. And, Daddy, it is delicious."

Daddy just smiled.

I gave him some moments to let that idea sink in.

By the time we got to the edge of the fields, the moon was shining so bright the path looked like it was glowing. Like the moon was showing us the way home.

So I just pointed. And Daddy nodded his head like he knew what I was meaning.

Once we were on the path I said, real quiet, "Daddy."

"Yes, Ida B."

I stopped walking.

When Daddy saw what I was doing, he stopped, too, and waited.

"I think the earth takes care of us, too."

Well, Daddy looked at me kind of surprised. He stood there for a bit, rubbing his chin and considering.

Finally he smiled and nodded and started

walking again, and I came with him, and he said, "I think you're right, Ida B."

And we were quiet the rest of the way home, just enjoying the breeze that was blowing through the stars.

❧ Chapter 5 ❧

This is what I eat for breakfast every single day: hot rolled oats with raisins and milk, no sugar. Even in the summer. Especially in the winter.

Every once in a while Mama will ask me, "Don't you want a little variety, Ida B?"

Now, when we get up, most times it's still dark outside. Sometimes at breakfast I'm so tired it's all I can do to keep my head propped up by my arm on the table. And I only open my eyes to make sure the oats are on the spoon and heading toward my mouth, but I close them while I chew. I am not ready for deep thoughts or surprises.

So when Mama asks me that I say, "It's too early for variety, Mama."

This is what I have for lunch every single day: peanut butter on one slice of bread, milk, and an apple, preferably a McIntosh because they're tangy with a thin skin, which Daddy says resembles me at times.

"Don't you want to try something different, Ida B?" Daddy will say.

Well, by lunchtime I'm wide awake and I've already been busy doing my chores and learning and having some fun. I've got a list of things that I can't wait to do in the afternoon, my head is filled to the rim with interesting ideas and plans, and that's exactly how I want it to stay.

"There are too many things to think about in this world besides what I'm going to have for lunch, Daddy," I say, and he looks at me like I am a true mystery.

This is what I have for dinner every day: whatever Mama and Daddy are fixing, and lots of it. Unless it's lima beans or brussels sprouts.

Mama and Daddy might ask, "Would you like some more, Ida B?"

And most often I will say, "Yes, puh-LEEZE." Especially if it's dessert.

Otherwise, at dinnertime we just chat about the day and what we want to do tomorrow and they ask me questions like, "What is the verb in the sentence: Mama reluctantly served Ida B another slice of pie?" or "Ida B, can you spell 'rambunctious' and use it in a sentence?"

And I answer. Unless, of course, my mouth is full.

Now, talking like that at dinner might

seem kind of strange, because I've been at other people's houses for meals and they don't ask each other "What planet is closest to the sun, dear, and would you please pass the potatoes?" Mouths full or not.

The reason we talked like that is because up until last year I was home-schooled. That meant I'd get up in the morning with Mama and Daddy and help with the chores. Then Mama and I would learn math and science, like the eight-times tables or the parts of a plant or "Ida B, if I give you twenty dollars to go to the store to buy some flour . . ."

And before she could get any further I'd say, "Which store?"

"It doesn't matter."

"Well, am I walking? Because I think it's too far for me to walk to the store in town and carry a big sack of flour back with me."

Then she'd frown at me and say, "Oh, Ida B,

now let me finish," like I was seriously trying her patience.

But I wasn't being a cause-for-a-headache on purpose. It just seemed like she was telling me a story about me and I wanted to know for sure what was happening so I could make a plan. Because I'll tell you something else about myself: I believe good plans are the best way to maximize fun, avoid disaster, and, possibly, save the world. I spend a lot of my time making them.

So then Mama'd say, "Let's start again. Billy Rivers's mother gave him twenty dollars to go to the store——"

"Who is Billy Rivers?" I'd ask.

"Nobody real. Just pretend."

"Then could he be a girl instead of a boy? And could she be named Delilah? And could she have green glasses that sparkle——"

"Ida B!"

"Okay, then, go on."

She'd give me the rest of the information, I'd put the numbers down on the paper, and get the answer right about ninety-nine percent of the time. And Mama'd say, "Good job, Ida B, once you get to it."

Later on in the afternoon, Daddy would read with me in the big chair or we'd write stories. Most of the time, though, we would just be living like always, and talking about things, and then we'd make the solar system out of vegetables.

Or Mama would have me figure out how much change we should get at the checkout at the store, and I'd say, "Seven dollars and eighty-six cents."

"She's very smart," the woman at the cash register would tell Mama.

And Mama'd say, "Hmmm . . . " with only one side of her mouth making a smile.

It meant we'd read and talk about the rocks in our valley and the mountain, and how they've been around for so long and they change so slowly and they were here way before us and will go on after us, too. Then, when I'd go and put my cheek against the big rock that sticks out of the side of the mountain and feel its warmth run into my body, I'd listen hard for its voice. When I finally heard it, it was like a low, gentle hum that went on and on, for all of time. And all that stuff I'd learned about rocks made sense, in my head and deep inside me, too.

Being home-schooled meant I didn't have to ride squished on a smelly old bus, or sit still in a stuffy room all day long. Mama made me take a test every year, and every year I'd pass with super-brilliant-flying colors. And I got to stay right where I liked it best: hanging around with Mama and Daddy, Rufus and Lulu, the trees and the mountain and the snakes and the birds. All day, every day.

It seemed like the best plan in the world to me.

✿ Chapter 6 ✿

When I was five years old, I went to school for two weeks and three days. I was in Ms. Myers's kindergarten class at the Ernest B. Lawson Elementary School.

Ms. Myers had pretty brown curls around her face and smiled a small sad-happy smile, where your mouth turns up but your eyes look pained, almost all of the time.

On the first day of school she stood in the doorway and said "Hello" to every one of us as we came in. She told each of us to find a seat on the big circle that was on the floor. So I did.

After everybody was sitting down, she brought a chair over and sat at the top of the circle and said, "Good morning, everyone. I'm your teacher, Ms. Myers. The first thing I need to do is to start learning your names. So when I call out your name, please raise your hand and say 'Here,' all right?"

We all nodded yes.

Emma Aaronson who, when she's in church, is always making her mouth move like she's singing whether she knows the songs or not, was first.

"Here," Emma said.

"Good morning, Emma," said Ms. Myers.

And Emma gave a "Good morning" right back.

"Ida Applewood" was next, and Ms. Myers looked around the circle to see who that might be.

"Here," I said, but I only raised my hand halfway, because that was just a part of my name.

"Good morning, Ida." Ms. Myers smiled and started looking for the next name on her list.

But before she could get away from me I told her, so we could get it straight right off, "It's Ida B."

Ms. Myers looked up, with a couple of wrinkles between her eyes. "Excuse me?"

"It's Ida B," I repeated. "My name is Ida B."

She stared down at her list again with an expression of deep pondering and some displeasure. But after a few seconds, that look of calm and sure delight people get when they figure out they're right and they're itching to tell you all about it spread across her face.

"Now Ida," she said to me, "I know that at home your family might call you by a nickname, like 'Ida B.' And that's just fine at home. But in this classroom, we're going to use our given names, not nicknames." Then she gazed around the circle with that sad-happy smile. "Does everyone understand that?"

And all of the kids nodded their heads and smiled right back except me.

"Now, let's continue," she said.

"Samuel Barton" was next, but I was stuck back at "Ida Applewood," and I stayed there for the entire list of names and "Good morning"s.

Because anywhere in the world we'd ever been, Ida Applewood was Mama. And any time I'd been around people for more than the little while and a bit it took to get to know somebody, I was Ida B.

So, I was wondering and worrying about how my head was going to remember to look up or say "Yes, ma'am," whenever Ms. Myers called out "Ida," when an even bigger problem occurred to me.

I realized that maybe having this new name that wasn't mine wouldn't just be for today or this year, but it might be my not-for-real-and-not-anything-like-me-but-I'm-stuck-with-it name for every school day for the rest of my life. That, I knew, was a whole lot of days of being Ida, and not being Ida B. So many days of being Ida that I might forget what being Ida B was like.

And with that thought a bad feeling came over me that started in my stomach and traveled out my legs and arms and ended up in my toes, my fingers, and even my tongue. Like everything was being tightened up and shrunk down and squeezed into a too, too tiny space.

I looked out the window and saw all of that sunshine and air and room to move, and I swear I could hear the brook calling to me, over that distance and through those closed-up windows. "C'mon home and play, Ida B. I'm waitin' for you. C'mon, c'mon, c'mon."

A powerful longing came over me to walk out of that room, go outside, and let that voice lead me home. But I'd promised Mama nine times just that morning I'd be good and follow directions. So I sat in my spot on the circle with my hands in my lap.

I kept thinking, though, that this was not anything like how Mama and Daddy had told me school was going to be, and I believed that was not a good sign.

There was a rabbit in a cage in the room, but we couldn't pet it until it was time. There were books on the shelves, but we couldn't read them until it was time. There was a big playground with slides and swings and balls, but we couldn't play on it till it was time. There were lots of kids, but we couldn't talk till you-know-when.

"Ms. Myers," I finally asked, "when is 'time'?"

"Pardon me?"

"When is 'time' for all of the fun stuff?"

"Well, Ida," she said, "there are different times for different things. I'll let you know when it's time for each thing. Why don't you just relax and enjoy the day."

Now, even when I was little, I liked to make plans. I wanted to know what was coming so I could stay away from the bad stuff as much as possible and get ready for the good stuff.

"Could you tell me now so I can make a schedule?" I asked.

Well, in one and one-half seconds, Ms. Myers was standing right over me. Her mouth was straight across and her hands were on her hips, and I've seen that look on grown-ups before and it has never meant anything good.

"Ida," she told me, "trust me. We will talk about a schedule when it's time."

And there were those words again. Right then I was wondering if I got in a class for bad children who needed fixing, and my punishment included losing my name and never being able to make a plan again. But Emma Aaronson was in the class, too, and she was every-minute-of-every-day-very-well-behaved.

I could feel a wallop of rude and ornery coming up my throat and fighting to get out of my mouth. But I had also promised Mama seven times while we drove to school that I would be polite.

"Yes, ma'am," I finally said through my teeth, because they were keeping the rudeness inside my mouth.

Then I made a schedule for the rest of the day with the only piece of information I knew for sure: what the clock would look like when it was time to go home. I kept staring at the clock over the door, watching the little hand get closer and closer to the three, until the bell rang for dismissal.

Mama was waiting for me at the edge of the parking lot at the end of the day, wearing a big smile.

Now, the real Ida B would have been grinning and running down to meet her. Ida B would have jumped in the truck, bounced on the seat five times, told Mama about her plans for the afternoon that would make her too busy to do too many chores, and rode all the way home with her forehead pressed against the window, she'd be looking so forward to getting there.

But I'd been Ida all day long. Ms. Myers's Ida, who sat still, stayed in line, kept her hands to herself, and didn't have a single, tiny drop of fun. I felt stiff and tired and cramped into a too-small body with a too-small name. So I just walked with slow, small steps to Mama.

When I finally got close, I stopped, looked up at her, and said, "Mama, this will not do."

"What will not do, Ida B?" she asked. And

when she said my name it was like I was back in myself for the first time that day. I felt my body loosen up and tingle, like it was waking up.

"Too many rules and not enough time for fun," I told her.

"Well," she said, "let's get in the truck and you can tell me about it."

So I sort of half-leapt into the truck. And on the way home I told Mama about the day: about Ms. Myers's pretty curls and her sad-happy smile, the invisible-no-kids-allowed-to-know-anything-till-it's-time schedule, the wonderful things everywhere that you couldn't touch or take time for, and, mostly, about Miss Myers refusing to use my real name. It took me almost the whole ride home to get it all out.

When I was done, Mama took a moment to think. Then she said, "Ida B, it sounds like a hard day. But there's always a lot to be done on the first day, and first days are usually not too much fun.

I'm sure tomorrow will be much better."

As we came to a stop at the end of the drive, I looked right at Mama and told her, "I highly doubt that."

But she looked back at me and said, "Give it another try, baby."

And it was so good to be home, with Rufus barking and running around in a circle, slimy stuff spraying out of his mouth every which way so you'd want an umbrella just to walk to the house, and the apples getting ripe so you could smell them in the air, and Mama smiling at me so sure, I said, "Okay, Mama."

But this is what I was thinking inside: While I surely hope you're right, I have a very bad feeling about that place.

Chapter 7

Just as I figured, things didn't get any better. If anything, they were worse. Because not only did we have all of those rules about not talking and not touching, but every day we were supposed to be getting better at following them. And every day I'd be slower and slower coming back to myself after school was finished.

"How many days to the last day of school?" I'd ask Mama in the truck.

"I don't know, Ida B. Why?"

"I just need to know."

"How many days until I'm done with school forever?" was all I could manage to get my mouth to say at dinnertime.

"Ida B, it can't be that bad," Daddy said.

And this is how low I was feeling: I didn't say anything back.

Then every night after dinner I'd go and lie down in the orchard till I got called to come in.

"What's the matter, Ida B?" Viola would ask.

"Nothing," I'd tell her, because I didn't have enough of anything in me even to complain.

"How's school going, Ida B?" I could hear Paulie T. snickering, because he was a punk way back from the beginning.

But even Paulie T. couldn't make things worse than worst.

Well, I guess I got so droopy and forlorn looking, Mama decided she wanted to see exactly what was going on in Ms. Myers's classroom. So the third week of school she came with me and visited for a day. And even though it was the same lining up and not touching and not talking and waiting my turn as always, it was better with Mama there.

School seemed to have the same effect on her as it did on me, though, because at the end of the day we both walked with slow, stiff steps out to the truck and didn't say a word the whole ride home.

When we got there, Mama said, "You can find something to do till dinner."

And I said, "Okay," because I knew when something was brewing and it was best to stay pretty still.

I sat down on the porch and I could see her go

find Daddy in the field, and they stood out there talking for some time.

The next morning we were all sitting down for breakfast and I was about to dig in when Mama said, "Ida B, Daddy and I need to talk to you about school."

Just like that, my stomach closed up like a trap. I stared down at all those little raisins that used to seem so happy bobbing around like they were swimming, but now it looked like they were drowning in a sea of milk.

"Look at me, Ida B," she said. So I did. "Starting on Monday, you're going to go to school here, at home, and Daddy and I are going to teach you. Now, we're going to have to get some information so we do this right. But we figure we've taught you just about everything you needed to know up till now, and you've been doing fine. So we're going to give it a try."

What did I look like right then? I must have been smiling, but I couldn't feel my face or my body. I was just hearing over and over again what Mama said, and I was floating up and up and music was playing and angels were singing, "Ida B is free, Ida B is free. Come fly with me, Ida B."

But before I flew off into the ether, I got pulled back down to earth by a heavy thought. This seems too good to be true, said the voice in my head that sees all of those presents on Christmas Day and knows that some of them are socks and underwear wrapped up in pretty boxes.

"No way, Mama," is what I told her, wanting to believe but not letting my hopes get carried away just yet.

"Don't think it's going to be easy, Ida B," she went on. "You'll have to learn math and reading, just like regular school. There will be tests and lots of work, and you'll have to do the things Daddy and I tell you. If we don't keep up and do what we're supposed to, you'll have to go back to learning at that school, understand?"

Mama was looking at me like I was right there in front of her, but I was taking off again. Because I knew as long as I was with Mama and Daddy and I was near the mountain and the orchard and the brook, everything would work out. As long as I could be Ida B, I'd be fine.

"For real?" I heard myself asking, and I had already floated all the way up to the ceiling.

"For real, if you do what you're supposed to," Mama said.

"No problem," I said back. But by then I was soaring in the clouds, so I don't know if she heard me.

That's how it went for four years, and it was finer than fine. I stayed home and I learned and I had more fun than a kitten with twenty balls of yarn and three pretend mice. I even started to believe that I could count on never going back to that particular Place of Slow but Sure Body-Cramping, Mind-Numbing, Fun-Killing Torture again.

And that, I would say, was a mistake.

❧ Chapter 8 ❧

In the morning, I'm like a snake in the spring: I need to lie out on a warm rock and let the sun sink into me for a while before I can start wiggling around and get on with the day. But Mama and Daddy aren't like that at all. They're like birds: they wake up before it's light, and they're singing and fluttering around just as soon as their eyes are open.

On the morning three days after that unreli-able punk Paulie T. had given me his not-to-be-trusted-in-a-million-and-a-half-years warning about trouble heading my way, though, there was none of the usual Mama and Daddy chirping or flitting about.

That day, some things were just like usual. I was awake, but hardly. The only things moving were my right arm and my mouth. *Get the oats, put them in your mouth, chew, chew, chew . . . get the oats, put them in your mouth, chew, chew, chew . . .* was the only message my brain was sending out, and even that was on slow speed and low volume.

But suddenly, I could feel my brain getting up to cruising speed faster than it had ever done at six A.M., and it wasn't because of anything Mama and Daddy were saying or doing. It was because they were silent and still, and my brain knew that that was unusual and just plain not right. I got a tingle down my spine, a funny taste in my mouth, and in about one and one-half seconds' time, I was wide awake and watching the two of them across the table from me.

Mama wasn't talking and she wasn't eating. She was just sitting there, playing with her food, which we're not supposed to do.

Daddy wasn't eating, either. He was just staring at his plate.

Then Daddy said, real low, "So you're going to call the doctor and make an appointment today?"

"Yes," she told him.

Mama smiled at Daddy too happy, too soon. "It's probably nothing to worry about, Evan."

Daddy, putting his hand over hers, said, "I know." But he didn't raise his eyes to Mama's. He just kept looking at the tips of her fingers sticking out from underneath his big hand.

There was a quiet in that kitchen I'd never heard before, like the whole world had stopped. And I knew that if I went outside right then, there would be no wind, the plants would have stopped growing, and the sun would be frozen in the sky.

"What's going on? What's nothing?" I almost-hollered, because somebody had to make enough commotion to get things moving and back to all right again.

Mama and Daddy looked over at me like I was a surprise.

"It's nothing for you to worry about, honey," Mama finally said. And Daddy looked out the window.

"What's nothing?" I repeated, because that sort of answer usually means there's more than plenty to worry about, but not too much that can be done. "Why are you sad? What's going on?"

But Mama just said, slow and somber like the wind on a rainy day, "Oh, Ida B."

Then she got up, cleared her plate, and that was that.

—

Here's the bad thing about being a snake in the spring: sometimes you find what you think is the best place in the world to sunbathe. It's the biggest rock ever, so long you can't see where it ends. And this perfect, so-good-you-almost-can't-believe-it's-true rock is smooth and dark and toasty warm. You slither out onto its snuggly warm blackness, and pretty soon you get so cozy and content lying there that you fall asleep, stretched out and snoring, even. You are sure you are in snake heaven.

But, being a snake, you're so low to the ground you can't see that this piece of rock paradise you're lying on is really a road. You're so cushy-comfy and sleeping so deeply that you don't hear that big old truck, hauling two tons of tomatoes, getting closer and closer.

And the next thing you know—*split, splat,* and a couple of crunches, too—there are tire tracks on either end of you. You're not sure exactly what happened, but all of a sudden you truly are gone from this world.

So, I've learned that even when you think you're in heaven, you need to stay alert and have a plan.

Some things are very hard to plan for, though.

Chapter 9

Mama had a lump. The lump had cancer in it.

That was the nothing that wasn't nothing, but it didn't seem like a too-terrible-everything at first. It seemed like a penny-up-your-nose kind of thing: you have to get it out because it doesn't belong there, and if you kept it there for too long, you'd have an awful hard time with a cold. So you go to the doctor, she takes it out real quick, and pretty soon you forget how it felt to have a sore, stuffed-up, stretched-out nose. That's how I thought it was going to be with the lump.

But it wasn't like that for Mama. First, she went to the doctor. After that, she needed to go to the hospital for an operation. Then, the cancer wasn't just in the lump, but under her arm, too. And the doctors hoped they'd gotten it all out, but they couldn't say for sure.

That cancer was like bugs in a tree: one day you don't see them at all and the next it seems like they're everywhere, eating the leaves and the fruit. And it won't work to find them and squish them one by one. You have to do something drastic.

So Mama went to the hospital for treatments, and when she'd come home she'd be so tired, she had to work hard just to say, "Hi, baby."

Then she'd go in her room and lie down on the bed. If you went away for an hour or so and came back, she'd look exactly the same: on her back, eyes closed, face white like milk, hands holding on tight to the spread.

I'd go to the side of her bed and stroke her cheek. "Unhhh," she'd moan when my fingers brushed her skin with a touch lighter than you'd use to pet a baby kitten. So I stopped touching her, but I asked her if she wanted me to read to her.

"No thanks, honey," she said, her lips hardly moving.

Did she want Lulu to come and visit?

"Maybe later."

Did she want to hear me spell "vivacious"?

"Not now, sweetie."

"Mama," I whispered once, when we'd both been quiet for a long time.

"Hmm," she replied, like she was answering me from a dream.

"Are you going to die?" I asked her so softly I could hardly hear myself.

Mama opened her eyes and turned her head

toward me. "Ida B," she said, looking at me more serious than ever.

"Yes, Mama," I said back, but I couldn't look at her, so I stared at the bumps on the bedspread.

"I will always be with you," she told me. "Always."

Then she turned her face back to the ceiling, closed her eyes, and said, "Do you understand, baby?"

And I said, "Yes, Mama," even though I didn't.

Then I just sat by her and watched her breathe, making sure her belly kept going up, then down.

Mama's hair started falling out in big tufts on her pillow, and I would go in her room and collect it when she'd get up for a while. I put it in Ida B's Bag of Assorted Things for Not Yet Determined Plans, but there was nothing in there except Mama's hair. I kept that bag under my pillow, and if I put my hand in it and closed my eyes, I could pretend I was floating in a cloud of Mama.

After Mama's treatments, our house would get as quiet as a library with only grown-ups in it. Like there was a constant "Shhhhh" hushing us all the time, in every room.

We walked around not looking directly at each other anymore. Daddy looked down, I looked down, even Rufus looked down. But not Lulu. She glared right at us as if to say, "Whatever is going on, I'd like my food five minutes ago."

We placed our dishes so softly in the sink. We pulled our chairs out from the table so carefully. We walked so lightly on the floors. I don't know if we were trying not to wake Mama or trying not to wake the cancer.

When there was time, Daddy and I would sit together in the big chair so we were close enough we could whisper and still hear each other, and read stories. And those were just about the only good times in the house then. Afterward Daddy would go and check if Mama would have some soup, or maybe some crackers.

"Do you want something to eat, Ida?" he'd say at the door to their room, and his voice was soft like rabbit's fur, light like smoke. It would float over to her and stroke her cheek, then her forehead, but never press too hard.

And most of the time Mama would whisper, "No thank you, honey." But sometimes she'd just say, "Evan," with the voice of a love that's a thousand miles away.

Mama would have a treatment, and things would be the worst.

Little by little, though, she'd start to get better, till she was coming close to being my mama again.

She'd start eating, and working with Daddy a

bit, and asking me, "Ida B, if it takes two and one-half cups of flour to bake a pie, and you bake two pies a week for one year except for the week of Christmas when you bake five, how many cups of flour do you need?"

"Only two a week, Mama?" I'd ask. "Couldn't it be three?" And she would almost smile, just like before.

But by then three weeks would be up and it'd be time for another treatment. All of the happiness that thought it might be safe to come back to our house had to turn around and go back to where it came from. Even the glowing that was Mama's disappeared from her eyes, and I couldn't find it no matter how long I looked at her.

Then, when no one was paying any mind, I'd go into my room, close the door, sit on the floor behind my bed, and cry and cry—for Mama and Daddy and me, and for all the love that seemed wasted because it couldn't fix Mama.

❧ Chapter 10 ❧

One day in August, the house and my heart got to feeling so gloomy and gray I decided to give talking to that old tree another try. I left Rufus home with Mama, hiked to the top of the mountain, climbed up the trunk, and sat in my usual spot.

"I don't mean to complain and I don't want to whine, but Mama's not Mama, and Daddy's not Daddy, and I miss them, and I miss the life we used to have, and I am so lonely," I told the tree.

I closed my eyes and rested my head on the warm, smooth branch next to me. I felt tireder than tired, so I was happy to just sit there for quite a while.

The sun was shining on my back, and the wind brushed my cheek like fingers. Then the hair on my arms and the back of my neck stood straight up and tingled, so I knew something was coming.

And I heard that voice that isn't an out-loud voice but you can still listen to it, just not with your ears. You have to hear it inside.

Slow like sleep, quiet like night, it whispered, "It will be all right."

And that was all.

There was a warm ball in my belly, and the warmth spread through me so I was heated from the inside out. Every bit of me got peaceful and warm and sure, and I forgot everything except for that feeling of being so sure.

Pretty soon, though, the part of me that's suspicious of things that feel too good too fast remembered all of the trouble and sadness that had been going on in our house. And the warm, cozy feeling disappeared real quick.

I opened my eyes, sat up straight, and said out loud, "Are you sure about that? Could you tell me what you mean by 'all right'?"

But that's the thing about that old tree: you're lucky if you get anything; and if you get something, that's all you get.

So I sat there and collected myself for a bit. And after a while, I remembered what I'd heard, and how it felt, and I just knew.

I climbed down, and when I got back to the ground I leaned up against the tree, put my face right into its old, white trunk, and said, "Thank you."

Then I walked down the mountain toward home. Not feeling any less lonely, but a bit more hopeful.

At dinner a couple of nights later Daddy said, with Mama sitting right there, "Ida B, Mama's going to get some new medicine for her treatments, so she won't be feeling so bad afterward. Your mama's going to be doing better soon."

"Evan," Mama said right away, looking hard at Daddy. "Not all of that's for sure," she told him, and her face got softer while she was talking. When she finished, she put her hand on his.

Then she turned to me. "We're *hoping*, baby, that it'll be better. I'm going to start having treatments every week for a while, but the medicine won't be so strong. I shouldn't get so sick, and I shouldn't be so tired. But we'll just have to see."

Well, except for the "hoping" and "have to see" parts, I thought that sounded like big-time-celebrating news. Like having-pie-*and*-ice-cream news.

I could feel myself smiling so big that the ends of my mouth were almost up to my eyeballs. But

Mama and Daddy just had little smiles, where your mouth curves up in the middle but only halfway. I couldn't understand why we all weren't skipping the main course and heading right for dessert.

"That's good news, isn't it?"

"It's good news, Ida B," Mama said.

"So what's the problem? Why aren't we cele-brating?" I asked.

But I got that same old answer, "Oh, Ida B," that didn't tell me anything except I better quit right there, because I wasn't going to get anything else.

And I was grateful for a half-happiness in a house that had been so full of sadness, so I let it be.

The brook, as you know, is much more talkative than the old tree. I would even say it's chatty.

The next morning I ran over to the brook, and before it could start gabbing, I told it, "Hey,

Mama's going to get better and pretty soon everything's going to be just the way it was."

But the brook didn't say anything back.

So I told it again, even louder, "I said, Mama is getting better and good times are just around the corner!"

Still nothing.

I took my shoes off and splashed into the middle of the water and kicked around there for a minute to get its attention. "Hey, did you hear me?" I yelled. "Mama's getting better and it's going to be back to just about perfect around here real soon!"

Then I stood still to listen, every part of me cold, wet, and dripping.

After a minute, when I was just about to give up, I heard the brook reply, sadder and stiller than I'd ever heard it before, "It's not over yet."

And that's all it said.

❧Chapter 11❧

Daddy had to sell part of the orchard and some of the farmland to pay Mama's hospital bills. One day in September he took me out to the barn, sat me down with Rufus beside me, and told me about it. "It's two lots at the farthest end of the valley, Ida B," he said.

I thought about that.

"But that's part of the orchard. That's Alice

and Harry and Bernice and Jacques Cousteau," I told him, in case he didn't realize who he was talking about.

"Ida B," he said, like he was ready for me, "there's no discussing it. That's just how it has to be."

"What are they going to do with the land?" I asked.

"I suppose they'll build houses."

"And what will they do with the trees?"

"I suppose they'll cut them down."

"Oh no, Daddy! No!" In less than a quarter of a second, I was crying and sobbing and yelling all at the same time. "Can't we sell something else?"

"No, Ida B."

"Can't we move the trees?"

"No, Ida B."

"Rufus and I will get jobs!"

"No, Ida B!" Daddy's voice was getting louder and angrier, too. "And that's it!"

Now I have to admit that, at this point, I was not getting any calmer. "And what about the brook, and the mountain, and the rest of the valley? They don't get to build there, or play there, or anything else, right?"

"Well," Daddy said, "the brook and the mountain and the rest of the valley won't be on their property, but I'd like us to be friendly and share what we have."

"No, Daddy! Just no!" I yelled, and I crossed my arms and shook my head back and forth with my eyes closed, my pigtails snapping in the air like whips. I was hoping one of them might give Daddy a good, sharp flick.

Daddy just let me sit there like that for a while, and I started to feel pretty dizzy, but I wasn't going to let him see me stop.

"Ida B, there's something else," he said.

Something else? That stopped the flicking and flapping in no time flat. But what else could there possibly be? I had to give Lulu away? Mama was dying after all? I sat still, with my eyes sticking out a couple of inches beyond the rest of my face, I was trying so hard to see what was going to come out of Daddy's mouth next.

"I can't take care of the farm by myself and teach you. And your mama's too tired to do much of any of those things right now. So you're going to have to go back to school. Starting on Monday.

"I know this is hard, Ida B," he went on, because I suppose he figured if he kept on talking, he could cut off the screaming and crying that were sure to be coming out of me, "but it's how it's got to be. You have to learn, your mama has to rest and get better, and I have to take care of the farm."

But this is how shocked I was: I didn't shout or holler or say a word.

The insides of my head started spinning, and pretty soon everything around me was tilting and turning. I checked to see that my feet were still setting on the floor, because it felt like I was falling down a hole that had opened up right underneath me. My stomach got queasy and I was sure that my lunch was about to make a repeat appearance, when my brain remembered the one thing that might save me.

"Mama's not going to let you do this," I said, trying to focus on a fuzzy, whirling Daddy.

"Ida B, your mama agrees with me," he told me back. "This is what we need to do."

And then everything went dark. My body was still sitting there, and my eyes were wide open, but the real me that feels things and talks and makes plans and knows some things for absolute one hundred percent sure had instantaneously shrunken and shriveled up and gone and hid way deep down inside me. I couldn't see anything except blackness, or hear anything except a kind of ringing, and all I felt was emptiness every-where around me.

I don't know how long I sat there like that, but it felt like years and years of being alone, huddled up and hiding in the darkness.

I heard Daddy calling my name, sounding like he was miles away. "Ida B!" he was saying over and over, and even though I didn't want to hear him, I couldn't help myself. The more I listened, the louder Daddy got, till finally I peeked out from inside me, like I was just waking up. There he was right in front of my face, saying my name and looking sad and scared.

And then I was crying again, and Daddy standing there saying, "It's all right, Ida B. It'll be all right," was only making things worse instead of better.

"Daddy," I finally got out, between one sob and another.

"Yes, Ida B."

"Please don't send me back to school."

"Ida B, you have to go."

"But Daddy, I don't need to go to school," I pleaded. "I . . . I'll teach myself. I'll use the books and I'll teach myself, I promise. I'll, I'll . . . " I was willing to memorize every boring fact about Canada or any nation he wanted, in the northern or southern hemispheres.

"You need to be with other kids, instead of moping around here all day." Daddy was losing any sign of sadness or sympathy, his voice was getting louder and harder, and he was not budging.

"I don't want other kids. I just want you and Mama and to be here. Please, Daddy. Please."

Well, I'll confess to you that at this point I was not just begging with my words. I was on my knees on the floor, with my hands clenched and lifted up to him, the way people look in pictures when they're pleading for mercy. But this Daddy was merciless.

"Ida B, that's enough!" he shouted, and the sound of his voice filled the whole barn. As soon as Daddy started yelling, my voice jumped back down my throat and my whole body froze up. Rufus was so scared he shot up like a bolt of lightning had run right through him. He went tearing out of the barn and was gone before Daddy's words were done bouncing off the walls.

Even Daddy looked surprised. His eyes got big, then he closed them tight. He put his hands to his forehead and left them there for a minute, then dragged them across his head till they grabbed each other at the back of it. He let out a big breath, like he'd been holding it in forever, and the barn was still.

With his eyes closed and his head bent down, Daddy told the floor, "Mama's sick and I'm busy and you're going to school on Monday. And that's how it's got to be."

Then he turned around, walked out of the barn, and went back to the fields like nothing had happened.

Chapter 12

After Daddy left, I was hurting something terrible, like every single part of me was cut and torn up. But my heart hurt the most.

I couldn't do anything except curl up like a ball on the floor of the barn and lie there, crying. The kind of tears that burn your eyes, and the sort of sobs that make your chest ache so that you're sure it's going to bust open. And when the sobs finally ran out, the tears kept coming, so I lay there with my mouth wide open, but I hardly made a sound. Just air going into me, and a heavy wind full of sorrow coming out.

But as I cried, my heart was being transformed. It was getting smaller and smaller in my chest and hardening up like a rock. The smaller and harder my heart got, the less I cried, until finally I stopped completely.

By the time I was finished, my heart was a sharp, black stone that was small enough to fit in the palm of my hand. It was so hard nobody could break it and so sharp it would hurt anybody who touched it.

I stayed there, staring ahead at nothing, with just about nothing left inside of me, for quite a bit.

And then my new heart came up with a resolution. Because when your heart changes, you change, and you have to make new plans. This resolution was for the new me, the new Ida B.

All right, Daddy, I thought, I'll do what you say. I'll go back to Ernest B. Lawson Elementary School. But I won't like it. I won't like the people who buy the land, and I won't like my teacher, or the kids in my class, or the ride on the bus. And I won't like you or Mama, either.

I decided I would do whatever I had to, just shy of death and dismemberment, to fight the craziness that had taken over my family and was invading my valley. I'd come up with a plan, and they'd be sorry, every single one of them, that they had to reckon with Ida B.

I could feel the hardness of my heart spreading into my arms and my legs and my head, and it felt fine. I would win.

That night I went up the mountain and stood in front of that bare, old white tree. "Thank you so much for your kind words of wisdom the other day," I said, sticky sweet like corn syrup. "I really took them to heart, I must say.

"Yep," I went on, like honey and brown sugar and molasses mixed together, "I have to tell you I was feeling much better after our little chat. I even expected great and wonderful things, thanks to your reassurance." I stood there smiling for a minute, giving that tree a chance to believe what I was saying.

Then I yelled, "You stupid old tree!" and I kicked its trunk as hard as I could so my foot ached something fierce, but I didn't even whimper. I limped back down the mountain and went to bed without saying good night to anyone.

And that was the end of me listening to anybody or anything, other than myself and my new heart, for a long time.

☙ Chapter 13 ☙

Things happened pretty fast after that. Sunday night I got my clothes ready for the next morning: black jeans, black T-shirt, black socks. And if I'd had black underwear, I'd have worn that, too. Daddy packed my lunch, and Mama asked me if I wanted ribbons in my hair tomorrow.

"No, thank you," I said, without even looking at her, because I would not dress myself up just so

I could be dropped, headfirst, into the Sacrificial Pit of Never-Ending Agony. But I didn't say that part.

I went to bed and after a couple of minutes Mama knocked on my door and asked, "Can I come in?"

"Okay," I told her.

She sat down on the edge of my bed and just looked at me for a while, but I stared at the ceiling like I was seeing something of the most supreme importance up there. She leaned over, put her hand on my head, and started running her fingers down my hair. I decided I was not going to enjoy that particular feeling at that particular time.

My heart distracted me by reminding me, over and over again, "She broke her promise. She agreed with Daddy. They're sending you back." And that did the trick.

Pretty soon, I felt a *plunk, plunk, plunk* on my

pajama top, and there was a wet spot in the middle of my chest. I looked at Mama, and she had big tears rolling down her cheeks and onto me.

"I'm sorry, Ida B," she said.

And, in spite of my rock-hard heart and its resolution, I felt a lump of sadness coming up from my chest into my throat. Somehow, a whole flood of tears had snuck back into my head while my new heart was preoccupied, and they were pushing at the back of my eyes.

I was done crying, though, especially in front of Mama and Daddy. My new heart told the sadness and the tears, "No, you cannot come out! Go back to where you came from!"

But sadness is a powerful foe, maybe harder to keep down than happiness, and it was a struggle. My throat ached and my eyes felt like they might explode, but I just kept telling it, "NO! NO! NO!" and eventually I could feel it retreating, little by little.

And I will admit that, even though I'd decided not to like Mama anymore, it was hard seeing her sadness. A part of me wanted to help it. But I knew if I said anything or touched her or moved just a bit, all the sadness in me would take that opportunity to rise right back up again and pour out, and there'd be no stopping it. We'd be lost in it forever.

So I just looked at her.

Finally she bent down and kissed me and said, "Good night, baby," and went away.

❧Chapter 14❧

"The bus stops at the end of the drive at seven thirty sharp, Ida B," Daddy said at breakfast the next morning, even though he'd already told me that three times the day before.

"Hunh," I said, which sounded more like a growl than agreement, but not so much to get me into trouble.

"Ida B . . . " Mama started twice, but she

never finished. And I just let it lie.

After breakfast I brushed my teeth, got my bag, walked out to the stop, and waited. I went out way ahead of time so I didn't have to talk with Mama and Daddy, so I didn't have to hear anything even closely resembling, "It will be all right."

It was raining and windy, but I left the umbrella Mama'd put out for me closed up in my bag. That rain soaked my legs and pelted my face and my eyeballs till they hurt, but I was glad because it just made me madder and more determined to be full-blown ornery by the time I got to school. And when the bus pulled up, I got right on without turning to see if Mama was waving from the window or Daddy was watching from the barn.

"Good morning," said the bus driver, smiling and cheerful.

"Morning," I said back like metal: cold, hard and flat.

I walked up the steps and paused at the top of the aisle. I made my eyes into slits so I'd look as mean as I felt. But when you make your eyes into slits, everything gets blurry, so everybody on that bus became blurry nobodies. Nobody I wanted to know, anyway. I walked down the aisle like that, not seeing anybody, just checking for a spot.

About halfway down, I found a seat all to myself. I sat there for the whole ride, squinting at the back of the seat in front of me with laser eyes, my mouth ready to growl, my hands like sharp claws gripping the bag in my lap, not thinking anything except, I *hate* this, over and over again.

Ten other kids got on the bus before we got to school, but nobody sat with me. I must have radiated foul meanness of the most terrible kind. Like there was a dark cloud of rank, revolting air around me that no one wanted to penetrate for fear of excruciating pain or agonizing injury.

When we got to school I filed off the bus and into the building with everybody else. Then I followed the signs to the office and stood in front of a big wooden counter.

"Can I help you?" asked a lady I might have thought looked nice if I wanted to believe anybody here was nice, and if I could actually see her, since my eyes were still like slits.

"I'm Ida Applewood," I said back.

"Well, Ida Applewood, what can I do for you?" Even with my blurry vision, I could tell she was smiling. You could tell it just from the sound of her voice. I hated it.

"I'm new," I said, and you could tell by the sound of my voice that her happiness had not infected me.

"Then let's see where you belong."

"I belong at home," is what my head wanted to say, before my new hard heart got a chance to quiet it. All of a sudden, I could see home and

smell it and feel it, and I missed it something terrible. But before I started blubbering and babbling everything to her, my heart stopped me. It
reminded me that even if I didn't belong at Ernest
B. Lawson Elementary School, I didn't belong at
home anymore, either. And I got mad all over
again.

"Here we are," she said, like she was telling me something pleasing. "You're in Ms.
Washington's class. That's Room One Thirty.

"Now, to get to your classroom," she went on,
"you go out this door, take a left, and it's the third
door on your right. It will say Ms. Washington,
fourth grade, on a sign outside the classroom.
Can you do that?"

"Yes, ma'am," I said, with just a bit of nasty in
my voice.

Because at that moment, as I turned to go
down the hall toward the Dungeon of Deadly
Dullness that I was sure awaited me in Room 130

of that school, I was overfilled with misery. I needed to release a little bit of it before it got to dangerous levels and burst out of me in the form of a wicked vileness that lashed out at anything in its path, including innocent kindergartners.

"You have a great day, Ida!" that woman called after me.

But I didn't say anything back. The less words the better, I was thinking, for everyone concerned.

Chapter 15

I stopped in the doorway of Room 130 for a
minute, just taking it in so I could do like soldiers
do before a battle: assess the enemy, formulate a
plan, get armed, and attack.

Some kids were still hanging up their coats,
talking to each other, getting books out, making
happy sounds. Outside the sun was starting to
come out, and it was shining in the windows.

There were rainbows and pictures and big color-
ful words on the bulletin boards. There was even
a pretty rug at the far end of the room where
there were no desks, only shelves of books that
looked like real books, not schoolbooks. All that
was missing were bluebirds and chirpy music.

And there was Ms. Washington, I figured, sitting in a kid's chair with her chin resting in her
hand, listening to some girl who was picking her
fingers and talking at the same time.

I could tell this was a warm place. Not a
warm temperature place, but a warm-feeling-
inside place. Some part of me knew it, but my
heart refused to feel it.

So I kept looking around, making a list of
everything in my head so I could use it if I had to
for my plan to be unknown, uninvolved, and
uninterested.

"Well, hello," I heard a low, friendly voice say.

I looked over to where the voice came from,

and there was Ms. Washington staring right at me and heading straight for me. That woman was like a truck: big and powerful and directed. But she moved smoothly and soundlessly, like a top-of-the-line luxury model.

"Are you Ida?" she asked, smiling as she came toward me.

And I was so surprised by her, by her voice and her size and that I could feel her even when she was twenty feet away, that I just stood there for a bit. When I gathered myself together, all I could do was nod.

"Welcome, Ida. I'm Ms. Washington," she said, and she put out her hand to shake mine.

I gave her my hand, not because I wanted to, but because I wasn't thinking straight. Ms. Washington turning out to be nothing like I expected had temporarily disrupted my assessment of the enemy and my plan, but not for long. I watched my hand go up and down like a pump handle.

"Why don't you take off your coat and hang it up, and then I'll show you around," she said.

So I headed to the coatroom and had myself back in fighting form by the time I got back to her.

"Everyone, this is Ida Applewood, and she's going to be in our class from now on," Ms. Washington told the kids in the room.

"Hi, Ida," they all chimed.

I stood there and gave them the blank-faced, Miss-America-the-Miserable-flat-hand-up-and-back-down-again wave.

"Why don't you each tell Ida your name and something about yourself," Ms. Washington said.

There was a girl named Patrice who had a sparkly shirt, sparkly fingernails, and sparkly barrettes, too, and said her best friend was Simone. There was a boy named Calvin who told me his favorite thing in the world was homework, and then he grinned real big at Ms. Washington. And there was a girl named Claire who said she liked to read and play with her friends and go on trips with her family and she would show me around if I wanted.

There was a whole bunch of other ones, too, and they were all smiling like they were happy to meet me and happy to be there, and it was all I could do to look at them and be polite.

"You poor suckers," I wanted to say, and I don't usually use that sort of language. "You just don't know any better. But I know the deal."

"Ida, is that the name you go by, or do you have a nickname you like to use?" I heard Ms. Washington ask.

Now I knew Ms. Washington was talking to me, but I couldn't believe she was asking me that particular question. Like she was trying to tell me that all of those tribulations with Ms. Myers were just a bad dream, that this bright, cheerful place was what school was really like, and tomorrow it was going to rain silver dollars, too.

She looked so sincere and caring I almost

wanted to almost believe her. But I didn't. And I wouldn't in a million and a half years.

"No. Just Ida," I said.

"Is there anything you'd like to tell us about yourself?" she asked me.

Well, there were a few things my mouth was itching to share. But I quickly decided that saying, "I hate school and anything that goes with it. And I completely expect that being a student in this class will suck the life out of me before the end of this week," on the first day back at Ernest B. Lawson Elementary School probably wasn't the best plan, even though it might be the most truthful.

"No, ma'am" is all I said.

"Well, all right," Ms. Washington said back, sounding a little disappointed but not pushing it. "Let's begin."

And it was all okay. Not good, but not the most terrible, excruciating, utterly painful experience ever.

Nobody bothered or picked on me. They smiled at me and I just looked straight at them, my face blank like they weren't even really there, which is the most effective technique for making people uncomfortable and ensuring that you will have no friends.

I did the worksheets, lined up, followed directions, answered when I was called on, didn't talk out of turn, and it was just fine. Better than being buried in an anthill with a boa constrictor around your neck and lima beans stuffed in your mouth.

At recess we went outdoors. I sat on the steps just outside the back entrance, put my chin on my knees, and watched nothing.

One of the girls from my class, the one named Claire, ran over, stopped in front of me, and asked, "Do you want to play with us, Ida?"

"No," I said right away without thinking about it, because that was my plan: no friends, no play, no smiling, no happy.

"Okay," she said back, looking surprised and maybe hurt, and walked away.

And I did feel a little bit bad about not even trying to be nice. But I knew I was right because here's the thing: how do you run and play when you feel like there are bricks of the heaviest sadness weighing down every part of your body? How do you laugh and talk when there are no laughs left inside of you?

Just when I'd been sitting on those concrete steps for so long my back end was numb, Ms. Washington came over and sat down beside me, so close I could feel the warm coming out of her. I could smell peanut butter and summer flowers on her, too.

"How's it going, Ida?" she said, matter-of-fact, looking straight ahead just like me.

"Okay."

"Anything you want to talk about?" she asked.

I stuck with my standard response. "No, ma'am."

"Well," she said, "when you want to talk, I'm ready to listen." And while I do believe that statement is number five on the top-all-time-silliest-things-grown-ups-say list, Ms. Washington didn't sound too silly when she said it.

Ms. Washington gave me a minute to soften up and give in, because she didn't know about my heart and its resolution, and that she was dealing with a mighty and unbending will.

"I'll see you inside, then," she finally said, after a good stretch of silence. And she touched my arm as she got up. Just enough so I felt it after she was gone, but not so much that I minded.

"Yes, ma'am," I replied.

Chapter 16

The Yellow Prison of Propulsion dropped me off just where it had picked me up that morning.

"See you tomorrow," the bus driver hollered as he closed the door behind me. And that was the worst thing he could have said.

I was full up with foulness again.

As I stood there at the end of the drive, though, I realized I'd been so busy thinking about school all day, I hadn't spent any time planning for what I'd do when I got home. All I knew was that I didn't want to talk to anybody, because I didn't have one nice thing to say anywhere in me. I did have a whole lot of things to say that could get me into trouble, though, especially if Daddy heard about them.

But there was no Daddy watching from the barn. And Mama wasn't at the stop or looking out the window. I was hoping she wouldn't be up and around when I got inside, either, because I knew that if Mama was there, she'd want to talk.

"How was your day, Ida B?" she'd say.

Then she'd look at me with those tired eyes, and even my foulness would be stilled for a moment. I'd stand there with my mouth closed tight, my lips zipped, glued, and stapled together to keep the angry words that were banging to get out and have a go at Mama from escaping.

But she'd ask me again, "Baby, how was your

day?" and my heart would not be able to pass up two invitations to have its say.

Those words would come shooting out of my mouth, heading straight for Mama. Words like, "What do you care?" and "You broke your promise" and "Have you seen my parents? Because mine disappeared and I'm living with two people who don't keep their word and don't care about me and are just plain mean." Words that would make Mama's eyes cry, and then maybe mine, too, and land me up to my armpits in the deepest pile of trouble ever.

I needed a plan for avoiding Mama, so I walked up the drive real slow to give myself a chance to come up with a good one. By the time I got to the front door, I knew what I would do.

"Hello," I'd say very politely if Mama was waiting for me. Then when she asked me how my day was, I'd tell her, "Could you please excuse me? I have a desperate need that must be taken care of immediately." I would cross my legs like you do when a certain kind of necessity strikes, make my face squinch up like I was about to burst, hobble up the stairs, spend three minutes and twenty-two seconds in the bathroom, and flush the toilet twice, even, to make it sound real. Then I would go to my room, and make a sign that read:

Mildly Sick
(but not so much she needs
her temperature taken)
Tired Child Inside.

Please do not disturb
until morning.

At the bottom, I'd draw a picture of Lulu sitting right in front of my door, baring her teeth and hissing, "STAY OUT, *please*."

That way, I wouldn't be telling any full-blown lies, and I wouldn't get myself in so much hot water that I'd be Ida B Stew by dinnertime.

I opened the front door just a crack and peeked around the corner to see what was waiting for me. But there was no Mama in the big chair or anywhere about. So I crept the rest of the way in, closed the door so quietly behind me, and tiptoed over to the stairs.

And just as I put my right foot on the bottom step, smelling freedom but not quite tasting it, who should come running out from the kitchen, jumping and barking and throwing spit every which way like he hadn't seen me in twenty years, but Rufus.

Every single plan I'd made went scampering over to the fireplace, shot up the chimney, and disappeared into the sky.

"Ida B?" I heard Mama calling from the kitchen.

"Yes, ma'am," I said back while I wiped my face with the back of my hand to remove some of

Rufus's slimy mouth juice and gave him a none-too-pleased glare.

"Come on out to the kitchen, honey."

"I need to go upstairs and get started on my homework" is what my brain thought would give me the best chance for escape, so I tried it out.

But another voice answered me back. It was the Deputy of Doom and Disaster. "Ida B, come to the kitchen," Daddy commanded.

And that was the end of hope. I put my head down and dragged my backpack behind me, getting ready for nothing good.

As I walked into the kitchen I could feel the two of them, one on either side of me. I decided I'd let them begin any conversing that had to occur.

"Are you hungry, Ida B? Do you want something to eat?" Mama asked.

"No thank you," I said.

"Honey," Mama tried again, "do you want to sit down and talk a bit?"

"I'm feeling kind of tired," I told the table. "And I need to use the bathroom," I added, saving a sliver of my previous plan. I started to turn around to get on my way.

"Hold on, Ida B," I heard the Master of Mercilessness say.

I froze, just able to see the hallway and my path to liberation out of the corner of my left eye.

"How was your day?" Daddy asked.

Well, it took me a minute to get over the shock that Daddy, of all people, would ask me that particular question. Especially since I was sure he did not want to hear Ida B's One Hundred Ten Percent True and Brutally Honest Response.

And now I faced a dilemma. I had to find a way to answer that inquiry without compromising my heart's resolution, while avoiding the temper of a daddy who would not appreciate anything sounding close-to-rude.

So this is what I came up with, which felt

better than any of my other options, but not any-where near fine: "It was okay," I said.

But in my head "okay" looked like this: O.K. Those letters stood for Outrageous Katastrophe, and I know it's the wrong spelling, but it was the best I could do at that particular moment.

Then I looked straight at Daddy and said, "Can I please be excused now?" and the words I used might not have been angry, but it was in my voice and flashing out of my eyes.

"Ida B . . . " Daddy started, already loud and pulling himself up straight. He was leaning for-ward so he could be a little closer if he needed to get ahold of me.

Mama stopped him, though. "Evan," she said, sad enough she didn't have to be loud, "let her go."

Daddy kept staring at me, but he leaned back after a minute or two.

And I walked pretty fast up to my room.

❧ Chapter 17 ❧

One night at dinner a couple of weeks later Daddy told me, "We've sold the lots, Ida B. To one family. And they're going to keep some of the trees."

"Maybe they'll have kids your age, baby," added Mama, who seemed to be doing better since she'd started her new treatments, but it was hard to tell since I was avoiding eye contact and word contact with both of those particular people. "Wouldn't it be great to have friends just down the road?"

"Great," I said in that way I had of talking then, a way that used words but didn't tell anybody anything.

That Saturday, the builders brought a bulldozer and a backhoe out to the land to clear part of the orchard and start digging the foundation of those people's house—those people I didn't even know, but I knew they didn't belong here.

Rufus and I walked down to the end of the valley and we sat in the woods and watched for a while. I squinted my eyes real, real tight this time, into the thinnest, meanest slits possible, and sent telepathic messages to the workers like, *Get away! You're at the wrong address!*

But as soon as they started cutting down the trees and plowing up their roots, my stomach got sick and my legs and arms got wobbly and my head felt dizzy. I had to get up and wobble-run home with Rufus looking at me, smiling and slobbering like he thought I was playing with him. It was all I could do to get to my room, lie down on the bed, and cover my ears with my pillow so I couldn't hear the cracking of the trunks and the grind of the machinery.

"I'm sorry, I'm sorry, I'm sorry," I said in my head over and over again.

When all of those terrible sounds finally stopped, I kept lying there, just like that, for a long time, sick and tired and numb.

And then my new heart came up with a plan.

Now up until that moment, ever since the day in the barn with Daddy, just about the only thing I cared about was putting together a plan to save me and my valley. But for all my wishing and hoping and sending out ten different kinds of prayers for a good one, not a single decent plan came out of me. It was as if all of the interesting ideas and exciting projects that had been running around in my head forever had just evaporated.

Because those first few weeks I went back to school, the only thing left in any part of me was unhappiness. It was the quiet kind, too, that doesn't do much and says even less. Every afternoon I'd come home, finish my homework, eat dinner, wash dishes, then sit in the big chair and do nothing.

"Ida B, what are you doing?" Daddy would ask.

"Nuthin'," I'd say, not bothering to muster the energy to say the word right.

"Well, why don't you find something to do," he'd tell me in a voice that didn't sound like merely a suggestion.

So I'd go and sit on the porch with Lulu on my lap, petting her but not paying any mind, so my hand was *thump, thump, thumping* on the top of her head. She'd get tired of that and give me a little bite to let me know that I was not giving her the attention she deserved, jump down, and walk away with her indignant tail up in the air as a final warning. Then I'd sit by myself, looking but not seeing, listening but not hearing.

Daddy would walk by on his way to the barn and say, "Ida B, stop moping and find something to do."

And I'd pick my body up and try to find somewhere else to go.

I couldn't go to the orchard. The apple trees wouldn't have anything to do with me. And they were always whispering things to each other like, "Did you hear about Philomena? They cut her down, poor thing."

"Who'll be next? What will those people do next?" they wondered.

"If I could, I'd pull up my roots and move to

the other side of the mountain, I would. This place is falling apart," the ones who didn't want to seem afraid would say.

But the worst was the sounds they made in the evening. "Ohhhhhhh, ohhhhhh," they moaned as the wind and their branches danced together in mourning, and their leaves waved good-bye to the spirits of their friends.

I stayed away not because they ignored me, though, but because I was afraid they would eventually speak to me. I was afraid they would ask me, "Why didn't you help us, Ida B? Why didn't you protect us?"

But I didn't have an answer, except that I felt like I'd been cut down, too.

So I'd sit up on the side of the mountain, grateful the stars were so far away you could barely hear their voices. Far away from the orchard and the brook and that old tree, until Daddy would call, "Ida B! Time to come in!"

Then I'd go home, get into bed, and do the same thing all over again the next day.

But now my heart had given me a plan. I had a mission, a purpose, and many, many things to do.

I'd rush through my homework and lock myself in my room till dinner, then hurry through dishes and disappear till the next morning. I was working toward nothing less than the righting of wrongs, turning evil to good, and stopping the craziness that was steadily and surely taking over my valley. I was Ida B, Superhero Deluxe, Friend of the Downtrodden, Foe of Cancer, Meanness, Mindless Destruction, and Traditional Schooling.

I drew a symbol for myself with the mountain in the background, and in the foreground were the remains of Ernest B. Lawson Elementary School. It was just a pile of rubble, and the only way you could tell what had been there was you could still put together some of the words from its also-decimated sign. I was suspended just above that heap of concrete, moments after its destruction.

My Super Assistant, Rufus, had cleared every man, woman, and child out of that building. In the next instant, I had flown straight down from heaven and, with one fist in front of me, rammed into the cupola of the school. With that single perfectly placed strike, I had pulverized the entire place. I was wearing purple pants, a purple shirt, and purple socks and sneakers. My braids were streaming behind me and I was smiling really big, too.

All around the school were apple trees, and all of the kids were safe in their branches, with Rufus, eating pie. The brook flowed past the ruins of that school, and in it were all of the teachers, the principal, and the secretary, too, wearing life preservers, on their way to Canada.

It was a tremendous drawing. I put it on the

back of my door and I didn't even try to hide it.

Next, I got on with the part to scare away the new people.

I made signs, posters, and notices in paint, marker, and crayon. In our encyclopedia, I researched the most dangerous and deadly things in the universe, and I brought them to our valley.

BEWARE OF POISONOUS SNAKES, one poster proclaimed, and there were pictures of some rattlesnakes, a cobra, and a boa constrictor squeezing the life out of a terrified woman, whose eyes were popping out of her head because of the pressure. At the bottom was a man, with two bloody fang marks on his ankle, whose life had obviously ended in agony.

TARANTULA SPOTTED HERE, announced another with the biggest, hairiest black spider standing behind the words, ready to grab you in its humongous pincers.

TORNADOES TOUCH DOWN WEEKLY, read a

third, with a picture of a twister carrying a cute little house, a mom, a dad, and two screaming children plus their dog off to who-knows-where.

DANGER: TSETSE FLIES; FEROCIOUS, RAVENOUS GIANT MALAMUTE ESCAPED FROM PET STORE AND SPOTTED IN VICINITY; PLAGUE OF LOCUSTS EXPECTED THIS YEAR warned some of the others, with very descriptive pictures.

I knew that some of these things would never occur where we lived, but I was hoping our new neighbors weren't so well educated. I used lots of big words to make them sound true, and I signed every one of them with the police chief's name, Vernon Q. Highwater.

They were masterpieces of terror.

When I had about forty of them done, I took my flyers to the building site of the new house, and I posted them everywhere—on the telephone poles by the road, on the trees that remained on the site, on the concrete of the foundation. I even taped them right to the framing that was already up.

And I started collecting things and leaving them as presents in their basement: snakes, spiders, grubs, and slugs. This place was going to sound so bad and scary, and look so disgusting, they'd want to stay in their house in town and never come live out here. They'd *give* the land back to Daddy, just so they wouldn't have to worry about an outbreak of bubonic plague or orchard-inhabiting alligators again.

❧Chapter 18❧

Back at school, Ms. Washington was trying to wear me down.

Every day at recess I'd sit on the steps. Every day she'd come sit beside me and say, "Anything you want to talk about, Ida?"

And every day I'd say, "No, ma'am."

But it got harder and harder to say, "No, ma'am" without looking at her, acting like she was a stranger, like it was really true that I didn't have anything I wanted to talk about.

When somebody stops to talk every day, and asks you about yourself, and doesn't say anything to fill your part of the conversation, just lets you choose if you want to fill it yourself, then it's hard to think that somebody's your enemy or to keep her so far away from your heart. It's hard not to trust somebody like that.

And she was wearing me down in ways she probably didn't even intend to.

Ms. Washington would read to us every day after lunch, and her voice was like ten different musical instruments. She could make her voice go low and deep and strong like a tuba, or hop, hop, hop quick and light like a flute.

When she'd read, her voice wrapped around my head and my heart, and it softened and light-ened everything up. It put a pain in my heart that felt good. When she told stories it made me want to tell stories. I wanted to read like her, so I could have that feeling anytime.

Ms. Washington would read good books, too, not silly ones where kids just learned how to behave right. The kids in her books did fun things, brave things, magical things.

She'd walk by my desk and set a book on it. "I thought you might want to read this," she'd whisper.

And I'd just leave it there, like I wasn't one bit interested. Then I'd slip it into my backpack at the end of the day. I'd take it out in my room at home with the door locked, and she was right—I did like it. A lot. But I wouldn't tell her.

I practiced reading out loud like Ms. Washington to Lulu and Rufus, but I did it in my room and quiet so Mama and Daddy didn't hear me. Rufus closed his eyes and looked so happy and peaceful, like I bet I looked when Ms. Washington was reading. Lulu got bored fast and started scratching at the door to get out, but I didn't care and I didn't take it personally.

I just loved making words into stories by the sound of my voice.

"Ms. W." is what I'd started to call Ms. Washington in my head, but never to her face, after a couple of weeks in that classroom.

On a Wednesday during silent reading time, I peeked over my book to see what she was up to. And there she was, with her chin in her hand, tapping her pencil on her desk, and staring straight back at me. As soon as she saw me looking, she smiled, got up from her chair, and started toward me.

Now, I know what somebody looks like when she's putting together a plan. I could tell that woman was cooking up a big one, and I was the main ingredient. And I wasn't going to have any part of it, because that was what my heart had decided.

Real quick, I turned myself forward again and put my book up in front of my face, so I would look like I was too busy to be disturbed. But Ms. W. was on a mission, and she wasn't going to be disappointed.

First, she sat next to me, and I brought my book so close to my nose, they were almost touching.

Then, she moved her head next to mine and, real quiet, she almost-whispered, "Ida, I need your help with something." And I got that good tingle up my neck and down my arms so the goose bumps come out, because she was making soft sounds next to my ear like my mama did.

"I need you to help Ronnie learn his times tables," she said, like a cat purring. "Do you think you could work with him? Teach him the way you learned them."

Well, it was like she'd charmed me and I couldn't break the spell. My hard heart wanted to turn to her and say, cold and sharp, "I'd prefer not to, Ms. Washington," snap my head back to forward, and that would be that.

But instead I just kept feeling her voice in my ear and all over. And I was nodding, not making any sounds like "Unh-hunh" or "Yes, ma'am" that might interfere with the memory of that soft voice asking me so kindly for something. That reminded me of what it felt like to be loved.

❧ Chapter 19 ❧

Ronnie DeKuyper was small and blond and ran faster than anybody in our grade. He was almost always smiling, and if I was going to like somebody, I suppose it would have been him. He was real friendly, even when people were kind of rude, and he never picked on other kids. But he was bad in math.

Not in adding or subtracting, but in multiplication he pretty well stunk so much that every time he raised his hand or got called on, I just closed my eyes and waited it out, because I knew it wasn't going to be right. Sometimes I'd think, "Man, Ronnie, you need to hang it up." But he kept on trying, and I respected him for not giving up, even though it looked like a losing battle to me.

So I was supposed to sit with him during study time and show him how I'd learned the times tables. But I couldn't remember how I learned them, except that Mama and Daddy just kept saying them to me, and asking me questions or making me recite them, and I kept trying, and pretty soon I knew them all.

I could tell Ronnie was embarrassed that I was going to be teaching him, because the first time I came over to his desk he just looked down at his feet.

Now, I know it's hard to not do well at something, and I know it's hard to need help. So instead of not saying anything or waiting for him to say something, which would be my cold-hard-heart routine, I ended up saying "Hi." Because I felt awful seeing friendly, happy Ronnie the Fastest Runner looking so uncomfortable and feeling so bad about himself.

"Hi, Ronnie," I said as I sat down at the desk next to his, which was the only time I'd said "Hello" to another kid since I started coming there weeks ago.

I believe Ronnie was unaware of the greatness of my effort, though, because he just mumbled "Hey" back, and was still watching his shoe, like seeing it scrape along the floor was the most interesting thing ever.

Well, if this had been big-headed Calvin Faribault, who thinks he's too fine for his own reflection, I would say he was being beyond rude. But this was Ronnie, and he was just a good guy feeling down. My rock-hard heart swelled up a little bit, even though I didn't want it to.

I talked to Ronnie real quietly so nobody could hear us, and he wouldn't get any more embarrassed. "Wanna play a game?" I asked. "Wanna play a game, Ronnie?"

He looked at me, just halfway, to see if I was serious or teasing him or just plain crazy.

"What kind of game?" he asked.

"A brain game," I said. "It's like an obstacle course for your brain."

"I'm not too good at brain stuff," he mumbled, and went back to being fascinated with his shoe.

"Yes, you are, you just don't know it," I told him. "Ronnie, do you run a lot?"

"I run all of the time."

"I bet if I ran all of the time I could be as fast as you," I said.

"I doubt it," he said back, which got me a little peeved, but at least he was looking straight at me now and all of his shame was gone. He was getting ready to go.

"Anyway," I said, because I decided to let that last bit lie, "it's all about practice. We're going to have to practice for this game, and then we're going to play, and I'm going to beat the pants off you forever unless you keep practicing. If you practice, you might beat me sometimes. Do you want to play or not?"

Now, I knew that we were at the point where either Ronnie gets insulted, spits on my shoe and says, "Forget it," or he gets fired up and says, "Let's go." And I could see both ideas were going through his head at the same time, because he was looking at my shoe and moving his mouth around like he was putting together a big goober, but he was also scraping his shoe real fast across the floor like he was getting ready to hop to it.

"Okay," he finally said. "What are we playing for?"

"I don't know," I answered. "We could play for who gets to go first next time."

"Nah, that's baby stuff. Let's play for quarters."

Well, I liked that plan for two reasons. I liked that Ronnie was a competitor, because that meant he was going to try and this whole thing wasn't going to be as boring or pitiful as I thought. And I also liked it because I knew I was going to make some money.

"All right," I said, and I decided in my head that almost every time we played my game, I'd challenge Ronnie to a running race at the end of the day, so he could win his money back. Or some of it, anyway.

But our races would have to be in private so nobody would think I was having any fun.

Then I showed Ronnie what he had to do to practice.

We started with the easiest multiplication you can do, other than one times anything: the ten-times tables. First I showed him how every answer is just the number you're multiplying the ten by, with a zero after it. Then I made him write out the ten-times table a bunch of times, and I did it with him so he didn't feel lonely. We had to say the ten-times tables over and over again, backward, too. Then we quizzed each other with just the basics.

"What's two times ten, Ronnie?"

"Twenty. What's eight times ten, Ida?" Like that till we were all warmed up.

After two days of that, we were ready for Celebrity Challenge.

For Celebrity Challenge, you can be anybody from any time, even from stories if you want. Ronnie wanted to be Carl Lewis, the all-around track star. And I was Queen Elizabeth the First because she had red hair and she was queen of England without a king or prince or anything.

For this particular game, the first person to get twenty-five right wins. In the first round, you ask each other just the basic times tables questions, but you can switch stuff around a little. You can ask, "What is twelve times ten?" but you can also ask, "What is ten times twelve?" In the second round, you can add or subtract a multiple, too, like "What is ten times ten, minus two times ten?" If you need a sudden death tiebreaker, you can be very complicated, but you have to be fair.

You're not supposed to use paper, but I let Ronnie use it the first couple of times. And I did beat the pants off him, too. A lot.

But, over time, I could tell he was practicing at home because he was getting better and trickier. Sometimes he'd want to play even when we weren't in study time, like when we were lining up to go outside and he thought he'd come up with a particularly sly question.

"Hey, Ida," he'd say, "a quarter for one question. Just one question for a whole quarter. Come on."

But most times I wouldn't even talk back to him because I didn't want other kids thinking I was hanging around with anybody.

The only way Ronnie could beat me was if he went first, and every once in a great while he did it. But I never beat him at running, even though I got closer, so it was fair.

I'd race him at the end of the day, while everybody was waiting for their buses, if nobody was paying any attention. We'd sneak out behind the school and run from the first yellow line on the playground to the back fence. Then I'd give him a quarter, and we'd walk back to our bus lines acting like we didn't know each other at all.

And I almost had fun with Ronnie. But I'd never tell myself he was my friend, because I met him at Ernest B. Lawson Elementary School.

❧Chapter 20❧

One day after lunch Ms. W. told the class, "I know it's time to read, but I don't think I can do it today. My voice is too tired."

She put her hand on her throat and scrunched up her face like something was paining her. It was the same face she'd make when Simone Martini was just about yelling across the room to Patrice Polinski, and Ms. W. would say, "Simone, use your inside voice. You are hurting my ears."

Everybody looked up from their chattering or worksheets at just about the same time, in exactly the same direction, with the same expression on their faces: a mix of thirty percent shock, twenty percent disbelief, and fifty percent plain old sad.

"Aw, man!" Matthew Dribble said right out loud.

I felt like the bottom had just dropped out of my stomach and everything I ate for lunch was tumbling around in my gut.

"Nope, my voice is just too tired," Ms. W. said, and, sure enough, it was sounding weak and raspy. "And we were going to read *Alexandra Potemkin and the Space Shuttle to Planet Z*, too. Well, that's disappointing."

Ms. W. sat down, put her head in her hand, and her body wilted. Like not only was her voice tired, but every bone in her body needed a rest.

"Please?" begged Alice Mae Grunderman.

"Please, Ms. Washington?" asked Patrice and Simone at the same time, with the same moon-eyed face.

And then everybody got the idea, and it became a sort of song with a verse of "Please, Ms. Washington" and a chorus of "Please, please, please."

But Ms. W.'s voice was deteriorating at an alarming speed, because now she could only speak in a hoarse whisper, and everybody had to stop with their "please"ing just to hear her.

"I'm sorry, but I can't."

She paused, and we could all tell by the look on her face that she was thinking hard. So we stayed quiet to give her some room.

"Maybe," she said, looking up and forcing a weak smile, "we could have a guest reader, just for today?"

Well, it was hard to imagine anybody but Ms. W. reading, and we all just sat there for a minute.

Then one by one, people started nodding their heads and looking at each other and nodding more and smiling, because nobody wanted to miss story time, not even Tina Poleetie, who usually slept through it.

And after a couple of minutes of that, people started looking at Ms. W., nodding their heads real hard, sticking out their chests, and saying out loud, "I think that's a great idea" and "Yes, let's have a guest reader today," because they were realizing that maybe they could be the Guest Reader and Star Student of the Afternoon. They wanted to remind Ms. Washington that not only were they superb readers, but wonderful human beings, too.

Especially Calvin "Big-Headed" Faribault, who actually raised his hand, and I just knew it was to volunteer out of the kindness of his big, fat, big-headed heart.

But Ms. W. didn't even look in Calvin's direction. "Ida, since I know you've read the book," she said to me weakly, like it was her last request, "could you please read the first chapter today?"

Well, I was so shocked and embarrassed, sitting there with my mouth wide open, that I almost couldn't tell that all the other kids were staring at me with their mouths wide open, too. Making words into story music like Ms. W. did was the one thing I wanted to do more than just about anything in the world. But telling a story out loud in front of my class at Ernest B. Lawson Elementary School was nearly the last thing I'd want to do in my entire life. I was so confused about whether I should be happy or scared, I just sat there.

Ms. W. got up, walked over to me, put her face next to my stunned and frozen one, and whispered, "Ida, I need your help."

And there I was, hypnotized by that woman again. I was like a dog that would go fetch Ms. W.'s stick, even if it was in a snake's hole under a thorn bush that had just been sprayed by a skunk.

I looked at Ms. W., just scared now, because I knew I was going to do it but I didn't know how.

"I know you'll be great," she croaked.

And in my head I was already trotting off, looking for that stick, even though I could smell the stink and the thorns were pricking me.

"Do you want to sit there, or in my chair?" Ms. W. asked.

"I'll sit here," I mumbled.

She set the book down on my desk, brought her chair over, sat down next to me, put her head back, and closed her eyes.

"Whenever you're ready, Ida," she rasped.

Ms. W. had given me quite a few books to read already because it only took me one or two days at the most to read them, unless I was working on my Terrify the People Who Bought Our Land Project. *Alexandra Potemkin and the Space Shuttle to*

Planet Z was my favorite so far. It was Rufus's favorite, too, I think, because he was turning out about a quart of spit for every chapter of that book I read.

I got tingly in my fingers thinking about opening up the book and reading those words out loud, making my voice go high and low, rough and smooth, like I did in my room. But my legs were shivering like they were out in a blizzard, and my stomach was flipping forward, then backward, forward, then backward, thinking about all of those people looking at me and hearing my voice.

I closed my eyes, put my right hand on top of the book, and passed it lightly across the cover. It was cool and smooth like a stone from the bottom of the brook, and it stilled me. A whole other world is inside there, I thought to myself, and that's where I want to be.

I opened the book and got ready to read the title, but I could feel everybody's eyes on me, crowding me so there was hardly any air. The only sounds that came out of me were little peeps, like a baby bird chirping *Alexandra Potemkin and the Space Shuttle to Planet Z.*

Ms. Washington, with her eyes still closed, leaned over and whispered, "You'll have to read louder, honey, so everyone can hear."

"Yes, ma'am," I whispered back. I took a deep breath, filled my stomach up with air, and then made my muscles squeeze it out, so it pushed a big gust of wind over my voice box and out my mouth.

"Chapter One," I bellowed. My voice was so loud it surprised me, and I jumped back a little in my chair.

But nobody laughed. They were listening.

The book is about Alexandra, and her parents think she is quite difficult, but actually she is a genius who is assisting the also-genius scientist Professor Zelinski in her quest to explore the lost planet Z. Alexandra gets into some trouble, but really she is just a very focused person.

At first, I was worrying about all of those people watching and listening. But after a few minutes, I left that classroom and went into the story. I was in Alexandra's laboratory instead of at school, and I was just saying out loud everything I saw her do or felt her feel. I let my voice tell the way she did it and saw it and felt it.

And I was so looking forward to seeing what happened next, I forgot that I was reading. All of a sudden it was the end of the chapter and it was like I was snatched out of a dream and couldn't quite recall where I was. I looked around and saw I was sitting at a desk, there was a book in front of me, kids were staring at me, and slowly I remembered.

I glanced over at Ms. W., and she smiled and whispered, "Thank you very much, Ida. That was lovely."

I handed Ms. W. the book, and we got back to work and everything was just like always, except that Ms. W. had to write all the instructions on the board instead of talking them.

At study time when I went to Ronnie's desk, he looked right in my eyes and said, "You read real good, Ida." And this time it was me staring down at my shoes like they might disappear if I didn't keep watching them.

My throat got stopped up so I could hardly say, "Thank you."

Nothing was different except the warm glow that was in my belly and my arms and my legs and my head and wouldn't go away. Even on the long, cruddy bus ride home.

⚘ Chapter 21 ⚘

"*H*ow was school today, Ida B?" Mama and Daddy would ask me every day after I first went back to Ernest B. Lawson Elementary School.

And every day I'd say, "It was O.K.," which now also stood for Overwhelming Kalamity.

"Well, what did you do?"

And I would just tell them the facts, hard and cold like my heart. "We had English, then we had science, then we went to the gym . . . " with no ups or downs or any part of the real me in there.

It was the same thing every day, and it was so boring and old and dry like stale bread I couldn't believe they kept trying for as long as they did.

After a while, though, they gave up. They'd just say, "How are you doing, Ida B?"

"O.K.," I'd mumble.

And that would be it. I didn't think they needed any more words than that to let them know that there was nothing close to joy floating around inside me.

But this day was different. The good feeling I had from reading that story out loud had been growing bit by bit all afternoon, till it ended up being a full-blown happiness by the time I got home. I'd keep thinking about what I did, and how it felt, and the warm brightness in me would get bigger and stronger and shinier every time.

My legs wanted to skip down the drive

instead of walk. My mouth wanted to smile instead of scowl. My arms wanted to hug some-body instead of holding my backpack to my chest like a shield. My heart was horrified.

That happiness would not be satisfied staying inside me, either. It wanted to be shared. And it didn't mind who it shared itself with, including Mama and Daddy.

I could just imagine having dinner with the two of them and all kinds of good feelings spilling out of me. There I'd be, grinning and gabbing, and the next thing you'd know Mama and Daddy would be thinking that I had transformed into my old perky self, that school was the best thing that ever happened to me, and maybe everything had worked out just fine after all.

And that would not be acceptable.

I was not going to let that happiness compro-mise my stand that, even though good things might happen in the world from time to time, nothing was right in my family or in my valley.

So I tried to get rid of some of it before dinnertime by telling Rufus and Lulu about my Out Loud Reading Adventure. I sat them both on my bed, and while Lulu glared at Rufus with the deadliest disdain, I told them my story. Two thumps of Rufus's tail and a bored yawn from Lulu, though, didn't quiet that feeling down at all.

By the time I sat down to dinner, that happiness was doing somersaults of excitement in my stomach. It was jiggling with delight at the prospect of telling Mama and Daddy about my day. It was itching to talk about how pleased I was with Ms. W. and the stories she gave me, and reading *Alexandra Potemkin and the Space Shuttle to Planet Z* most of all. It even wanted to start chatting about Ronnie.

I tried to get away before any of the pleasure leaked out of me.

"I'm not hungry. Can I be excused?" I asked.

Daddy, however, was prepared to spoil my plan. "You need to eat your dinner, Ida B," he said.

"Eat a little bit, honey," Mama added.

Well, by that point my heart was beating extra hard trying to keep that happiness down and quiet, and it was losing ground fast. I realized I'd have to let some of it out so I could rein the rest of it in and get control of my insides again.

I focused on my carrots, lining them up with my fork vertically, then horizontally, then zigzag. And I released one tiny tidbit of cheer.

"I read a book out loud to my class today," I said, struggling to keep my voice low and even.

Daddy looked up and stared, like he didn't quite know what to do with a bit of conversation from me.

"Oh, Ida B, did you like it?" Mama asked, smiling at me.

I just nodded my head.

"What did you read?" Mama kept on.

"Just a book about a girl," I told those carrots.

"Did you know the book, or was that the first time you read it?"

"I read it before."

"Were you scared reading in front of all of those people, Ida B?"

I shrugged, like it was such a not-big-deal I could hardly recall. "Not really."

"Was it wonderful, baby?" Mama asked.

And as soon as Mama said it, I felt every drop of the goodness from reading that story. It flooded my insides, and I couldn't stop the happiness from pouring out of me.

"Yes," I said.

Then I looked right at Mama, for the first time in what seemed like forever, and she wasn't looking at me, but into me. She was pulling me to her with her eyes, like she used to do. All of a sudden I could see the light that was Mama's shining out of her eyes. I couldn't help smiling at it.

"Be careful," my heart warned me.

But I was having a hard time remembering that there was anything to be careful about. Because if I just looked at Mama's eyes, and not her bald head or her pale skin, I could tell that the part of her I thought had gone away forever was still there and glowing, only from deep down inside her.

The part of me that knew how good it would feel to be held and cuddled was yearning. But now, having those kinds of feelings scared me, too. Thinking about being close to Mama and loving her like that, and knowing that things would still be terrible, and then I'd have to get used to staying away from her and not liking her all over, would be too hard.

"That's enough," my heart told me, as gently as it could.

I looked back down again, away from Mama's glowing, and right then all of the pain from the past months was in me and around me.

I stared at my carrots, arranged them in an X, and that happiness was finally stilled and silent.

"Can I be excused now?" I asked.

"Are you sure you're done, Ida B?" Mama asked.

"Yes, ma'am," I told the table, and I slid quietly off my chair, out of the kitchen, and up to my room.

And it's funny, but telling Mama and Daddy just that little bit ended up being worse than telling them nothing. Being in the same room but talking to each other like we were on opposite sides of the ocean turned the best thing into the loneliest thing. I was missing the old Mama and even the old Daddy more than ever.

❧Chapter 22☙

That Saturday, the intruders came to visit. I was sitting on the front porch and I saw a strange car, a big white one, come down the road and turn left at the T, head down to the building site, and park.

I ran behind our house, around the base of the mountain, and through the woods till I was directly across from their partly finished house. I climbed an old maple named Norbert, who wasn't talking to me but wasn't giving me a hard time, either. I was surrounded by his leaves, and I sat up there so I could watch those people, but they couldn't see me.

They were already out of the car, looking around the outside of the house. There was a mom, a dad, a little boy, and a girl who was a bit taller than me and looked real familiar.

At first they were all walking around the house together, and the parents were saying things like, "Oh, Ray, didn't this turn out well?" and "We'll have to talk to the contractor about this," but I wasn't minding them. I kept watching the girl.

Then she turned around and I saw her face full on with the sun shining on it, too. I had to hold tight to that tree's branches to stay put when I realized who it was.

That girl was Claire, the one from my class,

the one who asked me if I wanted to play the first day I was back at school.

The parents headed to the far side of the lot, and Claire and her brother found the hill of dirt the bulldozer had made. They ran over there, climbed up it, and then tried to see how fast they could run down it without falling over.

They were laughing and looking around to see what other kinds of fun they could have, and the whole bunch of them were just plain happy.

Nobody, I could tell, was thinking that this land used to belong to somebody else, that there were trees that lived here that had names and were alive, and they got cut down so this house could get built. None of them was thinking that the only reason they were here was because my mama got sick. But I was.

When those kids were done climbing the dirt hill, they started wandering around on the land,

and pretty soon Claire spotted one of my signs on a tree.

"Look at that," she said to the little boy.

They both ran over, and she read it out loud to him. "Typhoons Known to Occur Here. Water Rats Abound."

"What's a typhoon?" the boy asked.

"It's like a hurricane. But I didn't think they happened around here."

They studied my sign for a couple of minutes, then the little boy pointed to part of it and said, "That rat is funny," and they giggled together at my rat's pointy nose and buck teeth.

I felt my temper go from a simmer to a low boil, just like that.

"Hey, there's another one over there!" Claire yelled, and they both raced over to look at it.

"I like this one better," he said.

"Me, too. That's a pretty good snake."

"Are there really snakes like that around

here?" The boy's eyes were big and he was ready to be afraid.

"NO!" She laughed. "These signs are jokes; they're supposed to be funny."

"Oh!" he said, and laughed, too. "Let's see if we can find some more!"

And they were off, like they were on a treasure hunt going from clue to clue, running and laughing and having the best time. They loved my signs. It was like I'd made a game for them, a Welcome to the Neighborhood Game.

I went from a low boil to a bubbling-over-the-top-the-lid's-hardly-on-the-pot furious one in about two seconds.

Now, you might think that knowing that this girl was in my class, and remembering that she tried to be nice to me, might slow me down or soften me up a bit. But it did just the opposite. For some reason, knowing that this girl was nice, and had friends, and liked school, and had a mom and dad and brother and they did fun things together, made everything a hundred times worse. Knowing that it was her who was building a new house on my land, and it was her who cut down the trees, and it was her who would be roaming around in my valley . . . well, I couldn't stand it. I couldn't stand it so much that I couldn't sit still and I couldn't stay quiet.

Claire and her brother got close to the tree I was sitting in, still giggling and talking, and right then I boiled over, and I couldn't have held it back if I'd wanted to. I jumped down out of the tree, my hands waving and my mouth yelling, "This is not your property! Get out! NOW!" And I stood there, my arms raised like a barrier, with my teeth bared and a ferocious expression on my face.

They were so surprised they both jumped, their arms went up in the air, and their eyes and their mouths turned into big Os. The little boy started to cry, and for a second a part of me felt a little bit bad.

But then my new heart told me, "NO! They're the bad ones! They're the invaders! We are not giving anything else away!" And the part of me that felt bad got shut right down.

Well, it seemed we were standing there like that forever. My hands were fists now, my knees were bent, and I could hear my breathing, hard and heavy like a fearsome beast. I was not going to move unless it was to attack.

Finally, Claire's face changed: her mouth relaxed, and her eyes got smaller and kind of sad. "Ida?" she asked, like a doe would talk if it could, gentle and soft and a little timid. Like a hand extended, palm turned up.

And there was that part of me again, the part that felt bad before, thinking it might get a word in. "Take it, Ida B," it said. "Take the hand extended."

But my hard, cold heart wouldn't have any of that mush. "NO!" it yelled. "Nobody gets in!"

And my body howled out loud, with my face raised to the sky, the fiercest, scariest yell I didn't even know I had in me. "YOU ARE NOT ALLOWED ON MY LAND! GO AWAY!" I slashed and jabbed the air with my fists, like they were just itching to pound something.

When I opened my eyes and looked at the two of them, the little boy just turned around and ran away. He almost fell right over because he was trying to run faster than his short little legs were able. And I almost laughed out loud, because that's how foul I was feeling.

But she was still standing there, staring at me.

I looked back at her, eyes like slits and my mouth in a sneer, and yelled, "What are you waiting for? Didn't you hear me? YOU DO NOT BELONG HERE!"

She looked right into my eyes with those doe

eyes, crying now, not leaving like she was supposed to. I started to think that I would have to do
something drastic soon, because I couldn't stand
there looking fierce and breathing heavy forever.

But before I got too worked up again, she
said, right to my eyes and my insides, "You're
mean."

And she turned around and walked away.

I stood there, fists tight, still breathing like a
bear, ready to holler all sorts of things at her like,
"Too bad!" or "That's right! Remember that, big
baby!"

But right in the middle of my chest, where
her doe-eyed look ended up, there was a heavi-
ness that slowed me down and stopped me up.
"I'm not mean. Really. Come back," that soft,
sappy part of me wanted to say.

My rock-hard heart wouldn't have any of that,
though. "Stop it!" it yelled, and there was no more
weakness or sad, sorry feelings allowed. I was the

Protector of the Valley, and there was no use for mushiness.

When I walked back to my house, through the woods and around the mountain, every step I took was heavy and horrible, stomping the ground. Every time my left foot came down, I said, "I." And every time my right foot hit the earth, I'd say, "won."

So all the way home my steps were beating the rhythm to those words. "I . . . won . . . I . . . won . . . I . . . won."

Chapter 23

I went to dinner that night all set for a tussle. I was feeling pretty confident after my victory that morning, and I was thinking I was ready to take on my most formidable foes: Mama and, especially, Daddy.

Maybe there was no going back to the way things were before Mama was sick. For sure, there was no bringing back those trees that had been cut down. But that didn't mean there was no use in those two people feeling miserable about the sadness and destruction they and their completely-unacceptable-and-breaking-their-word-in-one-hundred-places decisions had brought into the valley and to me. That didn't mean I couldn't show them that there was somebody in that valley and in that house who remembered what was right and good, and her name was Ida B. Applewood.

My cold, hard heart was in top form, and it was not taking prisoners, including sick ones, tired ones, or overburdened ones, in particular. It was only going to accept complete surrender, which included a promise, signed by all parties, that would be valid for eternity and beyond, that things were going to change around here right that very minute.

I had written the whole thing out that afternoon and had the document in my back pocket.

"We, the undersigned," it began, because I had looked that sort of thing up in the encyclopedia, "solemnly promise that there will be NO MORE:

selling of land,

cutting of trees,

killing of things,

or sending children to school against their will,

EFFECTIVE IMMEDIATELY."

There was space for our signatures, and the seal of Ida B's Completely Just and Forever Binding Legal Services in the lower righthand corner.

I'd planned a speech for Mama and Daddy, too, and I had it all memorized. It started with, "I'm going to tell you two something right now, so you better listen up . . ."

Once I had their full and undivided attention, I'd keep going with questions like, "Don't you people care that everything has changed around here, and it's gone from just about righter than right to a million miles beyond wrong?" "Don't you care that those trees got cut down and they're gone forever?" and "Does it matter to you one-half molecule that I am just plain miserable?"

I was going to finish with a squinty-eyed skewer, aimed directly at Daddy. "You said that we were the earth's caretakers," I'd say. "You said we were supposed to leave things better than we found them. I don't think those trees that got cut down would say you'd taken very good care of them, do you?"

Then, when the tears were flowing and apologies were coming at me from both sides, and Mama and Daddy were saying to me, "What should we do, Ida B? What do you think we should do now to try to make things right?" I would pull that document out of my back pocket.

We would all sign it with my red pen to signify blood, but not for real. And we could start talking about a plan to get things back to normal around here.

I was still hearing that "I . . . won . . . " in my head as I stomped into the kitchen, sat down, and served myself like always.

When we were all done passing and pouring, I cleared my throat to get it ready for an army of words to pass through it. I put my hands on the table, looked at those two people sitting across from me, and opened my mouth wide so the words could come out big and fierce.

And Mama cut me off.

"Ida B, your Daddy and I have something we want to talk to you about."

My mouth was still wide open, but now it was hanging there out of surprise and a little dismay, because I hadn't figured on an interruption.

"Ida B," Daddy said, "we've been thinking about the south field that's been lying fallow for a while and that it might be a good place to plant some more apple trees."

"We were thinking that we could clear and plant it, the three of us, maybe this spring when I'm feeling better," Mama said. "And that maybe you'd like it to be your orchard, baby. Just for you. It would be your land, your trees, your apples. What do you think, Ida B?"

Now, first of all, when you get as worked up as I was, it doesn't go away just because somebody else starts talking. And second of all, I could see the plan those two had cooked up together, and I wasn't going to eat a bite of it.

I wasn't going to pretend that planting new trees would replace the ones that got cut down. I wouldn't believe that Ida B's Brand-Spanking-New Orchard was ever going to make me forget about Bernice or Winston or Jacques. And their giving me a piece of land and some trees that I didn't even know yet was not going to erase the Months of Death and Demolition and Not Enough Love to Fill a Teacup that I'd been through.

In about one and one-third seconds, my brain turned that big long speech I'd spent all afternoon putting together into one sentence that came out of my mouth, loud and strong.

"There is no making up for the terrible things that happened this year," I said.

And I thought that would be all, but it felt so good saying it, I kept going.

"You can't bring back Winston or Bernice or buy me off with a new orchard," I said, my voice getting louder with every word. "And you can't make everything that's wrong right with a patch of land and some new trees." Now my hands were pointing and waving, and I got my eyes into the meanest slits I could manage.

Then I thought of the hardest thing I could say to them. "And how would I know you wouldn't sell the land anyway?" I yelled. "How do I know you wouldn't let those new trees get cut down, too? You already broke your word in about ten million ways when you sold the land and sent me back to school. So why should I trust you?"

And just like earlier in the day, I was breathing heavy and looking fierce, people were staring at me, and I wasn't quite sure what I was going to do next.

But Daddy remedied that dilemma for me.

He slammed his fork down so the table shook and the milk glasses jittered and I jumped in my seat. His hands were clenched in fists, his face was red, and you could just about see the blood running, fast, through the big veins sticking out on his arms and the sides of his head.

Without thinking about it, I was sitting up straight with my hands holding on to the side of my chair, just in case he decided that my presence was no longer needed in that particular room and he was going to help me to remove myself.

"Ida B," he said through his teeth without moving his lips, looking like he was talking to his plate but he was talking to me.

Well, when somebody's talking and his lips are not moving, it is not a good sign. I pushed my chair back and pointed my feet toward the door, in case they needed to start running in that particular direction.

Daddy took a deep breath. You could hear it go in through his nose, and he pushed it out through his teeth so it sounded like a hiss. Then he took another breath, and this one wasn't so loud. His color went from deep purple to medium magenta. He kept going with the breathing till his face got to light red, then bright pink, and he looked at me.

"Ida B," he said again, with his palms flat on the table now. "Since your mama got sick, sometimes I've been so angry, I thought I could yell so loud and for so long that the mountain would turn into a pile of little rocks. And sometimes I've been so sad, I thought if I started crying I might never stop."

Daddy paused, but it was just to get some more of those cleansing breaths. "None of us likes what's happened around here, Ida B, but we're trying to make the best of it," he went on. "If we stayed angry or sad all of the time, things would still be hard, but we'd be miserable on top of it." He looked down at his plate again, and Mama put her hand on his arm and started rubbing it.

I'd hardly moved an inch since Daddy had slammed down his fork. I was still sitting there like a marble statue of Distressa, Patron Saint of Dread and Dumbfoundedness: mouth and eyes wide open, arms and legs sticking out, and everything as stiff as a board.

Finally Mama broke the silence.

"We know it's been hard, honey," she said, looking at me but holding on to Daddy. "We probably should have talked about it more. I guess we all got caught up in our own troubles and worries, and figured talking about it wouldn't help you at all."

She smiled and put her palm on my cheek, like a cradle for my face. "I'm sorry there have been so many hard changes, Ida B. We did what we thought was best, given the circumstances."

Now, a part of me knew that those people who were my mama and daddy were trying their hardest to make things right. A part of me knew that they were telling me that they cared—about those trees, about the land, and about me. That same part of me knew that there was something called love sitting just across the table from me, a hug if I wanted it, and talking and trying and warm feelings in the next moment if I'd just say, "All right." Even if I only whispered it.

That part of me was too small now, though. And my heart had made it go live behind my left knee, so it didn't get much say.

But my cold, hard heart did. It told me, loud and clear. "Do not let those people in again."

So I looked straight at Mama and Daddy,

pushed back my chair, and put a thousand miles between us.

Without asking if I could be excused, I stood up, turned around, went to my room, and shut the door tight.

"Good job," my heart told me. "You won again."

But I woke up in the middle of the night with a terrible ache coming from behind my left knee. And it stayed with me for the rest of the weekend.

Chapter 24

Even if you win a battle, as long as the enemy's got a heart that's beating and a brain that's working, you'd better be prepared for a counter-attack.

So, for the rest of the weekend and the whole bus ride to school on Monday, I was getting ready for Claire and retribution. Claire was smart, she had friends, and she was going to find some way,

I knew, to get back at me for scaring her and her brother.

Now, I don't need to explain what happens when a popular and persuasive young woman, like Claire, decides she's going to go after a solitary, no-friends-to-speak-of, somewhat rude young woman, like myself, at a place like Ernest B. Lawson Elementary School. Depending on how clever and cruel Claire was, and how much pain she thought I deserved, I was looking at a period of misery and mortification that might last a week or, maybe, the rest of my life.

I tried to think of every possible thing Claire might do, especially the worst, most excruciating ones, and figure out how I could either avoid total pain and humiliation or, at least, convince myself that it wasn't really that bad.

"She might call you a name," I warned myself.

Then I imagined her saying things to me like, "Smells like Ida brought the country to school with her. Do you feed the pigs, or do you roll around with them, too, Ida?" in front of about twenty other kids.

I practiced saying to myself, "I don't care. I don't care if Claire says I stink in front of twenty kids. I don't care if they all laugh at me and make up bad names for me."

And in my head I just turned around and told her, over my shoulder, "We don't have pigs, Claire."

I imagined Claire accidentally-on-purpose tripping me as we lined up to go inside from the playground, so all of the classes going in and all of the classes going out saw me lying on the ground, flat on my face, with my arms and legs sticking out like a four-legged starfish, blood pouring out of my knees and elbows and a bump the size of a melon coming out of my forehead.

"I don't care if everybody thinks I'm clumsy," I assured myself. Then I pictured myself being very careful and looking out for extended body parts wherever I went.

I imagined about two hundred seventy-six different things Claire might do to me and how I might protect myself from utter and complete degradation in all two hundred seventy-six cases.

Nobody, I thought, outplans me.

When I walked into the classroom on Monday, I kept my head straight ahead like nothing was going on. But I scanned the room from the corners of my eyes, back and forth like a minesweeper, for Claire the Vengeful.

I spotted her at her desk, and just at that moment the sides of both of our eyes met, locked, registered that the enemy was now within striking distance, and then looked away. I walked over to my desk. I discreetly checked my seat for sharp metal objects, then the inside of my desk for chewed bubble gum, worms, or rotting vegetables. Nothing.

I sat down and gave one eye and one half of my brain to Ms. W. and devoted the other eye and the stronger and more calculating half of my brain to the study of Claire.

But the first part of the morning went by without incident or even a hint of retaliation.

Claire didn't make faces at me, or whisper to her friends and point at me. The only thing that was different was she never looked directly at me. Her face was always turned away from me, like I was the scene of a gruesome accident she couldn't bring herself to even glance at.

By ten thirty I decided that she was saving her wallop for recess, where there's the least adult supervision, the ability to quickly assemble a mob, and many tools for injury. I used the rest of the morning to draw a map of the playground and plan multiple escape routes.

The safest spot was still my perch on the steps. If I sat a little closer to the ground, I could go forward, jump off to either side, or, if I had time to get them open, disappear behind the big doors.

Ms. W. did her usual check-in and I almost didn't hear or see her, I was watching Claire so carefully using my peripheral vision.

Then Ronnie stopped by and, for about the one hundredth time, asked me if I wanted to play dodgeball. And for the one hundredth time I answered, "No thanks, Ronnie."

But this time, instead of whispering it so nobody could hear me talking with somebody in a friendly way, I just said it out loud because I was so preoccupied. Ronnie sensed the change.

"What are you doing?" he asked.

"Nothing," I said irritably.

"You're doing something."

Now, if I was going to tell anybody anything, which I wasn't, it would have been Ronnie, I think. But if I told him one little thing like, "I'm watching Claire," I'd have to tell him many medium and big things, like why I was watching her and what happened over the weekend, too. And I wasn't ready for Ronnie to get to know that particular side of me.

So I just said, "Not now, Ronnie," and he looked at me kind of mad for a second and then walked away.

But it was better, I figured, to have Ronnie a little peeved than to have me a whole lot damaged and degraded, just because I'd let my guard down for three and one-third seconds.

Claire toyed with me for all of recess, pretending to be up to nothing. By the time we went back to the classroom, I was so tired from watching and planning, I just wanted to put my head down on my desk and take a nap. I supposed that a moment of weakness and fatigue on my part was exactly the invitation to injury she had in mind, though.

So I propped my head up on my arm, pinched my thigh about eight times, twisted it hard once, and stayed awake for the rest of the Claire-uneventful afternoon.

Her genius was beginning to dawn on me.

Claire didn't try to get me back on Tuesday, Wednesday, Thursday, or Friday, either. I was getting exhausted from watching and waiting and planning, and she wasn't revealing a single sign of a plot for my punishment.

If she was passing out papers, she didn't crumple mine or throw it on the floor. She'd just place it on my desk while she looked at the coatroom. She didn't write notes about me on the lavatory walls, leave slimy things in my jacket pockets, or have her mother call up my mama and discuss my behavior. I was confounded.

Truth is, I wanted Claire to retaliate. I wanted her to prove to me, Mama and Daddy, Ms.

Washington, and the universe-at-large that she was completely deserving of a little foul treatment, and more. I wanted to be reminded, often and obviously, that the world needed protecting from people like Claire, and it needed me to protect it.

Claire was not cooperating.

⚜ Chapter 25 ⚜

There was a little idea trying to get my attention, and it kept getting bigger every day, even
though most of the time I refused to pay it any
mind.

So it would wait till my guard was down and
sneak up to the front of my brain. Then it would
start out with small disguised-as-almost-friendly-
up-to-nothing-in-particular questions like, "What

if Claire isn't quite as completely evil and nasty as you thought, Ida B?"

But if I let that idea have any room and gave it any consideration, it would follow up with some bigger, harder questions that were just plain irritating. "What if," it would ask, "when you scared Claire and her brother, you were yelling at the wrong people about the wrong thing at the wrong time, Ida B?" or "What if you weren't a big, strong, righteous conquering hero that Saturday in the woods, Ida B? What if you went too far this time?"

And if I didn't cut it off right there, it would hit me with the big one, in spite of me letting it know it was unwelcome. "Ida B," it would ask, "what if Claire was right and you are just plain mean?"

I decided that I did not care to respond to that particular question at that particular time.

Just because you've made a thought be quiet, though, doesn't mean you've gotten rid of it. And this thought was clever. It was hidden and silent, but it was ready to attack the minute I left myself exposed. And it got me where I was most vulnerable.

Ms. Washington had decided that the guest reader idea was a good one, and she'd been giving other kids the chance to read, including the Big-Headed One. I liked the idea, too, though, because it meant that some day my turn would come around again, and I was itching to have another chance. But I didn't let her know that.

So when Ms. W. said, on a Tuesday about a week and a half after I'd done my part to save the valley from invasion, "You're about due for a turn reading, Ida. How would you like to read the next chapter of our book?" I'd had an answer ready for a long time.

"All right," I'd decided to say, not seeming too excited, but not leaving any room for confusion about my commitment, either.

That's what I'd decided, that's what my mouth was ready to say, and that's what my body was ready to do. But my brain did this instead: it thought about Claire.

It thought about that magic that happens when you tell a story right, and everybody who hears it not only loves the story, but they love you a little bit, too, for telling it so well. Like I loved Ms. Washington, in spite of myself, the first time I heard her. When you hear somebody read a story well, you can't help but think there's some good inside them, even if you don't know them.

And I figured the same was true for me. That all of those kids who didn't know me, and even Ms. Washington, who really hardly knew me at all, might think decent things about me just because I made my voice go up and down, slow and fast, soft and hard while I read. Just because I made that story come alive a little bit for them.

But I knew there was someone out there

who'd seen a part of me that none of the rest of them had. She would be sitting there, hearing my voice stop and start, slide and shake, and she would not be impressed. She would not believe in my goodness just because I could tell a story well.

"I saw the real Ida," Claire would say, "and she was cruel and selfish and bitter like lemon."

She knew I was mean. And all of a sudden, I did, too.

And I knew I couldn't read that day. Someone who has a cold, hard rock for a heart and likes it, who won't look at people or say "Thank you," who scares children and doesn't care if they cry, who doesn't mind if the whole world weeps because at least they'd know how it feels, too, well . . . Even if I could read the words out loud, and make them sweet and sour, long and short, high and low, all I would be hearing in my own head was "You're mean." And I knew I couldn't bear it.

"I can't. I don't feel well," I told Ms. W.

"Are you sure?"

"Yes, ma'am," I said to my feet because I couldn't look at Ms. W.'s eyes.

Ms. W. put her hand on my arm. "Another time then, Ida."

"Yes, ma'am," I whispered.

My head was so heavy I had to set it down on my desk, and my body got so cold I had to wrap my arms around it. My eyes were so tired I had to shut them tight, so there was just deep blue inside them.

Patrice read, and I was glad for the sound of her voice in the blueness. Not so much the words, just the voice.

❧ Chapter 26 ❧

On Wednesday at recess, Ms. W. sat down next to me on the steps, just like always. Just like always she asked me, "Anything you want to talk about, Ida?"

"No, ma'am," I said right away, because that's what I always did.

And thank goodness Ms. W. always stayed for a few extra minutes. Because I was thinking that if I didn't talk to somebody pretty soon, all that stuff I'd been holding inside of me was going to bust out screaming, bursting through my outsides so it could get some air and find an ear. There would be little screaming pieces of Ida B splattered across windows and in kindergartners' hair, and landing on top of you're-not-supposed-to-eat-them-outside sandwiches.

"Ms. Washington?" I said.

"Yes, Ida."

Both of us were looking straight ahead, like nobody would think we were talking.

"Did you ever do something that seemed right at the time, but later it seemed kind of wrong?"

Ms. W. was waiting. Like she was letting me have plenty of space to finish, just in case something important came into my head a little late.

"Yes, I have, Ida," she said after some moments.

And we both let the comfort of that settle into me for a bit.

Then I asked, "Did you ever do something because you were really mad, so mad and sad that you just had to try something to make things better, and it seemed perfect at the time but then later it felt a little wrong?"

This time Ms. W. waited even longer. But now, instead of liking her waiting, I was wondering if she'd realized that maybe she didn't want to be sitting so close to somebody like me.

"Yes, I have," she finally said, and when I peeked at her face out of the corner of my eye, she looked sad.

Now I took a pause, because the big one was ready to come rolling out, but I was afraid to say it out loud so someone in the world would hear it and know it and it would be real. My insides were still rumbling, though, and I knew I needed to say it or next thing it'd be Ida B's flesh-and-bone confetti raining down on the schoolyard.

"Did you ever do something because you were

so angry and upset, you were just boiling inside, and you had to let it out, and it seemed like a good idea at the time, but after a while it didn't feel so good? And what you did, well it . . . it . . . "—and now I was looking real, real hard at the blue house across the street, not even seeing a bit of Ms. W. at the edge of my eyeball—" . . . it made people cry, and they think you're mean." My voice was catching and cracking, so I let it rest for a second.

"And you didn't really want to hurt anybody," I went on, a little quieter. "You just wanted the bad things to stop."

I took a deep breath and looked down at my shoes, and everything else that needed to be said tumbled on out of me. "And after you did it you didn't tell anybody else, and now you feel like a sink that's backed up and it's full of dirty water and cat hair and old whiskers, and if somebody doesn't get the plunger pretty soon, that nasty old water's going to overflow onto everything."

Now, that was just about the longest question I'd ever asked, and it took me a minute to catch my breath when I was all through. As soon as those words were out of me, though, right away I had a better feeling than I'd had in a while. That space in my chest that my heart used to fill was feeling warmer and a bit more crowded than it had in a long time. And I liked it.

But I was also still scared about what Ms. W. might be thinking and waiting for her to say something. I was looking at her sideways, worrying a lot.

I watched her put her elbows on her knees. Then she put her hands together so they hugged each other. Her head dropped down, and she pushed the right toe of her shoe back and forth, just like Ronnie.

"Ida," she said, dark and slow like the water at the bottom of a river, "I have done something very much like that."

Well, I was so relieved, because Ms. W. understood and she was still sitting there next to me, that all of a sudden it felt like my heart was light and free and rising up and taking me along with it.

I only got about two inches off the ground, though, and then I landed right back on that concrete again. Because when I looked at Ms. W. full on, she was staring at the blue house, but her face was tired and sad and she looked about ten years older in ten seconds' time. She was remembering, and then I was remembering, too.

The sadness came back over me, and I knew I had to say something else or we'd both be stuck in that sadness with each other until at least the end of recess, and maybe for always.

"What did you do about it?" I asked.

Ms. W. looked at her clasped hands like there was an answer inside there if she could only get them to open up.

"Well, Ida," she said, low and calm and sure like the deepest knowing, "I just had to say 'I'm sorry.'"

And that was it.

That was all she said, all either of us said for the rest of recess. She sat there beside me, both of us looking out, blinking every once in a while, and I let what she said to me settle into my heart. After a couple of minutes, a peace rolled out from that place into every part of me, so even my head felt light and a tiny bit dizzy. When the bell rang we both jumped a little.

Ms. W. put her hands on her knees and raised herself up. "Well," she said, "let's get back in."

"Yes, ma'am," I said, standing up too, both of us still looking straight ahead.

We walked back to the room with her a little bit in front of me. I could feel the breeze her body made on my face, and I could smell peanut butter and summer flowers.

❧Chapter 27❧

Right away I started planning.

I would apologize, I decided, but I had not abandoned my resolve to avoid any possible pain or public humiliation at Ernest B. Lawson Elementary School.

That meant quick. That meant no friends, classmates, teachers, parents, brothers, or super-market cashiers nearby or within earshot.

It meant multiple escape routes and backup plans.

Now, say there were one million possible ways Claire could respond to "I'm sorry." And say fifty percent of those possible responses were kind, decent ones, like, "That's okay, Ida. No problem." Well, out of all of those thousands and thousands of friendly, cordial, or just plain tolerant replies Claire might give me, I could only think of three. And I didn't believe a single one of those three would happen.

I didn't have any trouble thinking of the bad responses, though—the ones where crowds laughed, body parts disappeared, or foul-smelling, rotting things kept turning up in my personal belongings.

"You're a snake, Ida Applewood," I could hear Claire say in front of a crowd of hundreds. "A slimy, green, sleazy snake. So go slither back to your hole and swallow some worm-filled mice that are carrying a deadly disease so you get it and your skin turns green and shrivels up, your eyes bulge out and explode, and you die the most hideous, painful death imaginable."

No, I had no problem thinking of the bad ones. And since most of the bad ones involved some kind of complete and horrible degradation in front of large groups of adults and children, my first priority was figuring out a way to get Claire alone.

But you're never alone at school. Never, except for maybe a couple of seconds. Definitely not in the classroom or on the playground, in the office, the auditorium, or the gym. Even in the lavatory, there's almost always a first grader with a small bladder who just has to go at the same time as you.

Only the custodian's closet promised privacy, but that meant stealing a key and kidnapping

Claire, closing the door without her screaming her head off, somehow convincing her not to tell on or pummel me, and fitting an apology in there, too. All in less than five minutes.

After carefully considering my options, I decided that the lavatory was my best chance for success. Only two people could go at a time. And if I could work it so those two people just happened to be me and Claire, and if, at that moment, the small-bladdered people just happened to be in the gym or the lunchroom, I might be able to achieve an instant of utter aloneness with her. Just enough for a quick "I'm sorry."

At the sink or, better yet, in the stall next to her, I'd say, with that metal partition between us, "Claire?"

"Who's that?"

"Ida."

"What do you want?"

"I'm sorry about the day in the woods."

And then I'd be done. She could slam the door, flush the toilet till it overflowed, spit under the partition. I wouldn't care. I'd have done what I needed to, and I'd be on my way back to the classroom.

❧ Chapter 28 ❧

If you're going to intercept somebody in the lavatory, you get, at best, about two chances a day: one in the morning and one in the afternoon.

On Thursday morning, Claire faked me out. We were in the middle of free time, when we could walk around the room without getting permission. So instead of raising her hand and asking, she went right up to Ms. W.'s desk, talked to her, and was out the door. By the time I realized what was going on, Judy Stouterbaden had asked, too, and we were at our limit.

The morning was a waste. I focused on the afternoon.

After lunch, during silent reading time, as soon as Claire's hand went up, so did mine. Waving a little so it couldn't be missed.

"Yes, Claire," Ms. W. said.

"Are we supposed to read the story all the way to the end, or just to the chapter break?"

That was not the question I'd hoped for. I yanked my arm down and shoved my hand under the desk so Ms. W. would forget it had been raised.

"To the end, Claire," Ms. W. said. Then she turned to me. "Did you have a question, Ida?"

Now, if I said "No," a clever Claire might figure something was up, and that would not be good. But I had not planned for this particular turn of events. I did the best I could.

"Um, I was wondering in what grade you need to know how to spell the word 'predicament'?"

Twenty heads turned to look at the person who would ask such a question. Twenty brains started turning that question into a big juicy teasing. Twenty bodies, I was sure, got ready to jump all over me as soon as I walked out the door at three o'clock. My efforts to avoid humiliation seemed to be wasted.

Ms. W. smiled. "I don't know that 'predicament' is on any specific spelling list, Ida. Why?"

Paralyzed, my face on fire, I could only look at her, shocked at what I had done. Ms. W., thank goodness, let it lie.

Still in that state of shock, I didn't even notice when, about two minutes later, Claire raised her hand, asked another question, and left the room. I was just starting to function close to something-like-normal again, when I saw her walk back in. And slowly I realized what had happened.

At 2:12 P.M., my last chance for reaching my goal on Thursday was gone.

On Friday, wherever Claire went, so did I, about eight and a half paces behind. While she browsed for books in the classroom library, I sharpened my pencil till it was just a point and an eraser. Every time she walked near Ms. W.'s desk, I got into the sprinter's start position: legs bent, right leg out front, feet ready to spring, arms ready to pump.

At 10:27, Ms. W. asked, "Ida, will you take this form to the office, please?"

Now this was bad timing. My body drooped and I gave her a look that said, "Do I have to?" without the words.

"Ida, please." She put her arm out to me with the form, and her head went back to her work.

As soon as I was in the hall, I ran as fast as I

could to the office, slowed to a walk ten feet from the door, dropped off the form, and ran back to the room. My head just about spun all the way around on my neck looking for Claire. Sure enough, just as I feared, she was gone.

I felt a little breeze across my back, turned around, and there she was, back from her morning trip.

Claire didn't go all afternoon. I watched and I waited, but she waited longer.

Twenty minutes before the end of the day I realized that I myself needed to use the bathroom. Badly. I'd been so focused on Claire that I hadn't noticed the pressure building, and there was no way I'd make it all the way home, thumping and bumping over ruts in the road, on that bus.

Ms. W. gave me the all-clear, out-with-no-waiting release. Then I did the speedy keep-your-feet-low-to-the-ground-so-you-don't-bounce-too-much shuffle down to the lav, took care of my business, opened the stall door feeling one hundred percent better, and shot straight up in the air.

Claire DeLuna was standing right in front of me, arms crossed, leaning against the sink. She was looking straight at me, waiting for me, alone, like I'd been trying to do to her all week. If I had been any less shocked, I would have turned around and locked the stall door, but I was petrified. I was the Statue of Surprise, the Venus of Dismay.

I had been outplanned.

"Why are you following me?" she asked.

My mouth, which had been hanging wide open, shut itself for a second, then gave up and just hung there again.

"Are you trying to do something else mean to me?" she said.

Well, I'd been so focused on getting Claire alone, and I was just so startled by her superior cleverness and that she thought my following her was to do something nasty, that I couldn't remember what I wanted to tell her.

As I stood there with my arms out, my head bobbing, and my mouth babbling, "I . . . I . . . I . . ." Claire turned away.

And as she walked out the bathroom door, she yelled back at me, "Just leave me alone!"

So there I was. A week of planning and trying my hardest and everything was worse instead of better.

It rained that afternoon and all evening, the kind of rain that stings when it hits your skin. And that felt just about right.

❧Chapter 29❧

Saturday morning, I was sitting on the front porch, waiting for nothing, with nothing I wanted to do. Rufus sat beside me for a while, hoping I'd be up to something more than misery. But he got tired of waiting and went off on his own, leaving a small sea of spit where he'd been sitting.

Just as I was about to take myself back to bed and try starting the day over again in the afternoon, I saw the big white car come down the road and turn left at the T. And right away, I knew what I had to do.

No plans. No least-possible-pain-and-humiliation scheming. Just plain and straight do the deed.

As soon as the white car disappeared down the DeLunas' drive, I picked myself up and headed out through the fields, then around the base of the mountain.

I walked through the orchard, eyes fixed forward, not slow and not rushed, either. Like I was on my way to the final showdown. Yes, there was a bunch of them and only one of me. Yes, they might ambush me, and I might not come back in one piece. But I'd take whatever those people needed to dish out, because I was going to do the right thing.

I stopped just before I stepped onto the land that now belonged to the DeLunas, and took a deep breath as I walked over that invisible boundary line.

And there was Claire straight ahead, looking at me, waiting for me. Her mom and little brother were crouched down at the side of the house, planting little bushes.

Clump . . . clump . . . clump . . . was the only sound my feet were making this time as I walked toward Claire, arms out from my sides and palms up, letting her know that I wasn't coming for a fight, even if she had some trouble and torture she needed to visit on me.

Claire's mother spotted me and stood, dusted off her hands, and watched as I walked up to Claire. Then all of the world was still except for the two of us.

"Claire," I said, making myself look her in the eye, "I'm sorry I scared you in the woods. I'm sorry I was mean to you. I was following you in school so I could apologize. I . . . I . . . " And there I was, babbling again. Should I tell her about Mama and the trees and school and everything? Where would I start if I was going to explain it all?

Then Ms. W. came into my head and I knew it didn't really matter.

"I'm just sorry," I said.

Sometimes, on spring days, there will be the brightest, warmest sun and the darkest, rainiest clouds sharing the sky. All day long you wonder, "Will it rain? Will it shine?" And that's what I was thinking then, while I was looking at Claire's face. Everything was there, but nothing was happening one way or the other. I couldn't hang around any longer to see what would win out, though, because I had something else to do.

I turned to Claire's little brother, who had his arm around his mama's leg, and I could see that he was scared of me. He thought I was a monster, just like I'd wanted him to.

"I'm sorry I scared you," I said. "I won't ever do it again. I promise."

And he just stared at me, too. If I didn't know better, I would have thought that this family's mouths were under repair.

It was too hard waiting there for those people to decide if they wanted to tell me something, and I wasn't quite sure I could stand to hear the words they might want to say anyway. So I turned back to the orchard and started home.

I braced myself for a DeLuna ambush from behind and decided that when Mama and Daddy found me, just holding on to a tiny sliver of life, my last words would be, "Turn the land into a park, teach Rufus some mouth-related manners, and make sure Lulu gets her treats. Please."

But I got to the property line without harm or hollering, and by the time I crossed it, I did feel better. Like my heart was heavier and lighter at the same time.

❧ Chapter 30 ❧

Apologizing is like spring-cleaning. First of all, you don't want to do it. But there's something inside you, or somebody outside you who's standing there with her hands on her hips saying, "It's time to make things right around here," and there's no getting out of it.

Once you get started, though, you find out that you can't just clean out one room and be done with it; you have to do the whole house or you're tracking dirt from one place to the other. Well, it starts to seem like too, too much, and you want to quit more than Christmas. But there's that somebody or something telling you again, "Keep going. You're almost done. No quitting allowed."

Then all of a sudden you are done. It was an awful terrible time, and you never want to have to do it again in your whole life. But it is kind of nice seeing everything clean and looking just right.

And at that moment you're almost glad you did it. Sort of.

So I had a good sleep on Saturday night, but when I woke up on Sunday morning, I knew I wasn't finished.

I walked out to the middle of the orchard and took a deep breath. My legs were shaking because those trees and I hadn't chatted in quite a while, and I wasn't sure how angry and maybe vicious they were going to be. There were a whole lot of them, and some of them could be quite rude, as you know.

"I'm sorry I couldn't protect your friends. I'm sorry I couldn't save Winston and Philomena and the rest of them," I started out. "Daddy says we can plant more trees in the south field, and I know that doesn't make anything okay, but we're trying." I knew that part wouldn't help, and it might even hurt me with them, but for some reason I wanted them to know that Mama and Daddy cared.

"I miss them, too," I said.

Well, all of those trees, hundreds of them, and not one of them said a word. I was beginning to think that my apologies made people's voices freeze up, and I would have to try that out on Emma Aaronson next time she started going on about how she's so good the angels had reserved a special spot for her sitting right alongside them in heaven.

But if you've ever talked to a bunch of people, and that bunch of people was some of your best friends, and they acted as if they didn't even hear you, like you weren't even there, you know how lonely that can feel. I guess I was just to my limit with feeling bad about myself, and lonely, and tired out in general. So I sat down on the ground and I cried.

And since those trees weren't talking to me but I figured they weren't going anywhere, either, I told them everything. I just let it all pour out of me, for the first time, I guess. I told them about Mama and the lump, Ms. Myers and my name, what I did to the DeLuna kids, what I said to Mama and Daddy. And how I'd missed those trees but figured they'd be angry with me, and I was afraid something exactly like this would happen, so I hadn't come to visit.

When I was all done, it was still quiet. For a minute I felt that awful fear you can get when you

225

think about maybe never, ever having somebody you love's company again.

But then Viola, who is the kindest of the bunch, whispered, "We missed you too, Ida B."

Maurice, who's about fourth nicest, said, "Welcome back, Ida B."

And right then, my heart almost overfilled with happiness.

Then that stinker Paulie T. said, "I'm still mad, and don't think I'm forgetting anything, Ida B. And I'm not too sure about forgiving, either."

"Oh, Paulie T.," said Viola.

But I was feeling so much better, I could deal with Paulie T. myself. "Are you going to hold a grudge?" I asked.

"I don't know," he said back, being the punk that he is.

"That's okay, Paulie T.," I told him. "But if you want to talk, I'm ready to listen."

Then I chatted with the nice ones for a bit,

and it wasn't like old times. But sometimes, when you haven't talked with a friend for a while, even if it's strange and stiff and you don't quite know what to say, it can still feel better than ever.

Before long it was time to go, since I had a few more stops to make on Ida B's Avenue of Atonement. I got all the way to the edge of the orchard before I realized I had something else I needed to tell those trees.

I turned around so I was facing all of them.

"I won't ever let it happen again," I told them. "I won't ever let it happen again, I promise."

And I headed over to the brook.

The brook started right in with so many questions I couldn't keep up. "Where have you been, Ida B? What have you been up to? Why haven't you stopped by? What's been going on?" And then it started repeating itself, so I interrupted.

"I'm sorry I haven't been by," I said. "I was busy and sad and that's no excuse, but I missed you and I'm back now, so don't worry."

Then I had to get going because the brook can keep you busy for a whole day just listening, and I had one more place I needed to go.

When I got up to the top of the mountain, I cleared my throat.

"Hello," I said. I stood there in front of the old tree, back straight, hands clasped in front of me. "You're looking well. How've you been?" I asked, just to get things going in a cordial kind of way.

But the old tree doesn't bother much with small talk, so I moved on with my business.

"I'm sorry I was rude. I'm sorry I was disrespectful. You were right, sort of, because it all did work out okay, but not perfect. I got mad at you, and I apologize for that," I said.

But those words were not doing the job. I was saying the right things, but not the really true things.

Because I'd done something to the old tree

that was just wrong, and that I didn't want to admit I would even think about doing. When I kicked that tree, I wasn't just trying to scare it; I was trying to hurt it. And I had a hard time imagining forgiving somebody who had done the same thing.

I stepped closer, talked quieter. "This is hard," I whispered.

My heart was banging in my chest so I could hear it in my ears and feel it in my fingers. I closed my eyes, took a deep breath, and filled myself up with the breeze from the valley. Then I let it out slow so it could get back to its travels, with a little bit of me added to it.

"I am sorry I kicked you. I am sorry I was mean. I am just so sorry," I said, right into the old tree's trunk.

And then I didn't know what else to say, so I just stood there for a very long time. Not listening for the tree to tell me something, but just to be there with it. Because it felt right.

The wind was blowing a bit on the top of the mountain, but everything else was quiet. And after a while, all of me got quiet and calm, too.

I felt alone again, but not in a bad way. I felt like I could grow roots and stand right there on the mountaintop for all of time and never be lonely again. Even if the old tree went away.

Then I heard a hum. It was coming from the tree. Just like when you hum and you can feel a quiver in your lips. Well, the hum from the tree made my whole body quiver that little bit.

And the tree told me something that my heart understood, but it wasn't in words. It was a knowing. But if I had to give it words, if I had to tell you what that tree said to me, it would just be this:

"Always."

That humming and quivering broke away the last little pieces of my rock-hard heart that I didn't even know were still there, and tears came out of my eyes, but I wasn't crying. I put the fingertips of my left hand on that old tree's trunk and felt the smooth, worn, warm whiteness.

"Me too," I said.

⚜ Chapter 31 ⚜

I suppose it would seem real nice if Claire and I got together on Monday and started chatting and playing dodgeball and decided we were twins separated at birth and would be best friends for the rest of our lives, living right down the road from each other. But we didn't.

I guess she looked at me more, or she

didn't avoid looking at me so much, and I wasn't watching her out of the corners of my eyeballs anymore. We'd even say, "Hi," but no names, if we ended up face-to-face with each other.

The good thing was, I didn't feel bad when I saw her. I was still sorry for what I'd done, but I didn't think I was due any torment and torture for it. If Claire wanted to, that was her business, but I wasn't looking for it.

At recess on Monday, Ms. W. stopped by my spot on the steps like always.

"Anything you want to talk about, Ida?" she asked, just like always.

"No, ma'am," I said. But this time I looked straight at her and I smiled.

She looked into my eyes, like she was checking to make sure that smile had its roots deep down inside of me. "All right then." She smiled back and moved on.

"Do you want to play dodgeball, Ida?" Ronnie asked me for the one hundred fourteenth time on the Thursday after Ida B's Weekend of Apologies.

Now I don't know why people like Ronnie keep on trying, especially with people like me who are so good at saying "No." And it almost makes me wonder if the part of his brain that had a hard time learning the times tables had a hard time learning when to take "No" for an answer. Mama would say he is persistent, and many days I found that quality of his burdensome. On that particular day, however, I found his perseverance to be something I was almost grateful for, if I let myself admit it. But I couldn't be too agreeable too quickly.

"Who's playing?" I asked.

"Just about everybody. See them all over there?"

"Whose team would I be on?"

"You can be on mine if you want."

"Is whipping the ball allowed?" I knew it wasn't, because I'd been watching those kids play for weeks, but I was pretending to be weighing my options carefully.

"No."

"If I don't like it, can I quit after one game?"

"Sure."

"What if the ball hits my shoe and the ground at the same time—am I out?"

"I don't know."

Now here's another thing about Ronnie and that quality of his. By that time, most people would have had enough of me and my questions and just moved on. But Ronnie hung on and he wore me out. I ran out of questions.

"Okay," I said, not letting my voice sound too excited.

And Ronnie's so smart in some ways, he didn't act surprised or happy. He just walked over to the game with me, but not too close.

And she got me out right away, Tina Poleetie did, because I'd never played dodgeball before, I guess. Something happened to me when I got out there, so I just stood there watching the ball come right at me and did nothing. It hit me in the belly and dropped down to the ground, and Tina yelled, "You're out!" and I went and sat at the side of the lot until that game was over.

But I did better in the second game. And by the end of recess I believed I could grow to become a dodgeball player of great skill and fame.

❦ Chapter 32 ❦

Friday night after dinner, Daddy was working in the barn, and Mama and I were doing dishes.

Mama was washing slow, and I was drying slower, like we were giving the dishes some room to tell us something if they needed to.

Mama set a plate in the rack to be dried, and then she just stood there. I dried that plate and then I dried it again, keeping busy till another came along.

"Ida B," Mama finally said.

"Yes, ma'am," I said back, still polishing the plate that was between us.

"Sometime . . . " Mama started. And then she stopped, like she was having trouble figuring out how to finish.

"Yes, Mama?" I said, while I studied the pattern on that plate like I was memorizing it for an exam.

"Ida B, " she tried again, "sometime . . . " and then she turned her body toward mine.

Well, it was like Mama's body was a magnet, making my body turn to her, too, and my eyes couldn't do anything but look to see what her eyes were doing.

And there was Mama, so close my skin was tingling like it expected to be touched. This Mama, who was different from the old Mama. She was slower and stiller, and even when she laughed there was a sadness around her mouth that never went away. But my insides knew her. And her eyes had that glowing, brighter than it had been in a long time. They were smiling, and wondering.

"Sometime, honey," she said, soft like footsteps in new snow, "I'd like to hear that story you read at school." Mama looked down and took a breath to fill herself up again. Then she came back to me. "Would you read that story to me sometime, baby?"

And then there was a silence between us.

Now, I knew that silence needed me to cross it. But even though Mama was right there, the space between us felt awfully wide, and getting across it seemed like a dangerous venture. I was thinking that I might want to spend some time putting together a plan to cross it without getting hurt.

But my new-old-big-and-filled-up heart told me that if I'd just take a step, without considering it too much, in an instant I'd be at the other side. So I did.

"All right, Mama," I said.

Mama smiled, then she turned around and got washing again. I put that plate away and got ready for the next one.

And the glowing traveled around the room and wrapped itself around us, one at a time and then together.

Just about the time Mama and I were finishing up, Daddy came in. He got a drink of water, looked out the window over the sink, walked around the kitchen table, looked out the window again, cleared his throat, and said, "It's a nice night out there."

"Hmmm," Mama said back, and touched Daddy's arm as she walked by him and headed over to the big chair.

Daddy kept staring hard out the window, like

he was searching for something of the utmost importance. Then he cleared his throat again and said, "Ida B, let's go for a walk."

Well, I hadn't been alone with Daddy in forever. And the idea of it made me a bit nervous, since the last time we'd had some all-by-ourselves time he'd told me they were selling the land and I was going back to school, and things hadn't gone too well from there. But I was still feeling the warm sureness from my time with Mama, so I said, "All right, Daddy."

I looked over at her and asked, "Mama, do you want to come?" thinking she might ease the strain of our togetherness.

But Mama smiled from where she was sitting. "I'm tired, baby. You two go on alone."

So we took the King of Slobberville and headed out, and we walked for quite a way with Rufus's panting and slurping being the only sounds any of our mouths were making.

When we got to the far end of the orchard, didn't Daddy look up at the stars, take a deep breath and say, "We are the earth's caretakers, Ida B."

Now, I have to admit that, after all of the terrible things that had happened and been done that year, I was a little surprised to hear Daddy saying that to me again. I was so surprised that even my feet got confused, and one tripped over the other. I was just about flying through the air, on my way to a not-too-friendly meeting with the ground and some good-sized, sharp-edged stones.

But before I went headlong into the dirt, Daddy caught me by the back of my shirt, pulled me right up, and set me on my feet. Then he planted himself down in front of me, looked in my eyes, and asked, "Are you all right?"

Daddy and I hadn't spent too much time looking directly at each other in quite a while, and I think seeing each other's eyes was a bit of a shock and a fascination to both of us. So the two of us stayed there staring, a little embarrassed and kind of mesmerized, for a minute or so.

And neither of us said a word, but I swear I heard my daddy speak. Like the old tree speaks. Not in words, but a feeling that went straight into my heart. But if I had to give that feeling some words, this is what I think it was saying:

"I'm sorry."

Well, it was like Daddy was just bursting with surprises. And this one was such a shock, I thought I might start falling over again, only backward this time. But the sadness and trueness in his eyes kept me standing straight and still, right there with him.

And then I sent a message back to Daddy. Not with words, just a feeling. But I let my body show him what my heart was telling him, just so he wouldn't miss it or get confused.

I put my hand on his shoulder and I looked

into his eyes as deep and hard as I could, till I could tell that the sorrow that was in there was paying attention. Then I nodded my head, twice. And that was it.

"All right, then," Daddy said as he stood up, brushed off his pants that weren't dirty, and turned around so we were both facing home.

We started walking again, Rufus leading, back through the orchard toward the house. And just as we came to the edge of the apple trees, I stopped and said, "Daddy?"

He stopped, too. "Yes, Ida B?"

"I think the earth takes care of us."

And didn't he rub his chin and look like he was pondering that thought, but not for quite as long as the last time we had that particular conversation. "I think you're right, Ida B," he told the sky and the stars and the valley, and then we headed on home.

As we walked, I could hear the trees behind us

humming agreement, "Mm-hmm," and I could feel them doing something like nodding their heads, if they had heads to nod.

I looked up at the mountain and saw the old tree glowing with the moon shining on it, and all of a sudden I felt filled up again, so that my heart might come up my throat. And I was thinking how that can come over you, out of nowhere, and if it wasn't such a fine feeling, it might almost be frightening. Like there's more love and good thoughts and powerful things inside of you than one body can hold.

"I'll be in in a minute," I told Daddy as we walked up the porch steps.

"All right, Ida B."

And I just sat on the porch looking at all of that land and the mountain and the trees and the stars that weren't mine at all, and never would be. But in some ways they'd always belong to me, and I couldn't imagine not belonging to them. It

245

doesn't make sense in words, maybe, but it made sense to me that night.

"Good night," I whispered.

"Good night, Ida B," a quiet chorus came back, riding on the breeze.

We care about the health of this planet and all of its inhabitants. So all hardcover editions and the first paperback edition of this book were printed on 100% postconsumer recycled paper (that means that no trees were cut down to create the paper). And that paper was processed chlorine-free, because when chlorine is used to bleach paper, the process creates toxic by-products called dioxins and furans that can make people and animals sick.

As a result of these choices, to date all printings of *Ida B* have also saved:

2,107 trees
(304 tons of wood)

768,289 gallons of water

98,659 pounds of solid waste

1.5 trillion BTUs of energy
(equivalent to one year of electricity required by 16 average U.S. homes)

185,095 pounds of greenhouse gases
(equivalent to the annual emissions of 17 automobiles)

176 pounds of hazardous air pollutants

Environmental impact estimates were made using the Environmental Defense Paper Calculator. For more information, visit http://www.papercalculator.org.

Acknowledgments

My most heartfelt thanks to:

My mother and father, who raised me, always, with books;

Aunt "Doreen," who supplemented with songs and stories of the strangest sort;

Carol Creighton and Mary Jo Pfeifer, the best of teachers;

Kate DiCamillo, Alison McGhee, and Holly McGhee, most marvelous readers, editors, and believers;

Lynn Lanning, RN, OCN, for her patient instruction and advice;

Steve Geck and everyone at Greenwillow Books and HarperCollins Children's Books, who have given *Ida B* such extraordinary care;

Catherine Dempsey and Angela Hannigan, grandmothers and namesakes, for the gifts of storytelling and a mighty and unbending will;

Victor Clark, who listened again, again, and again, with love, constant.